Our Kind of Love

Peregrine Bay
Contemporary Romance Series

SHIRLEEN DAVIES

**Book Two in the Peregrine Bay
Contemporary Romance Series**

Avalanche Ranch Press, LLC
PO Box 12618
Prescott, AZ 86304

Book design and conversions by Joseph Murray at 3rdplanetpublishing.com

Cover design by The Killion Group

ISBN: 978-1-941786-31-4

Books by Shirleen Davies

Historical Western Romance Series

MacLarens of Fire Mountain

Tougher than the Rest, Book One
Faster than the Rest, Book Two
Harder than the Rest, Book Three
Stronger than the Rest, Book Four
Deadlier than the Rest, Book Five
Wilder than the Rest, Book Six

Redemption Mountain

Redemption's Edge, Book One
Wildfire Creek, Book Two
Sunrise Ridge, Book Three
Dixie Moon, Book Four
Survivor Pass, Book Five

MacLarens of Boundary Mountain

Colin's Quest, Book One,
Brodie's Gamble, Book Two, Releasing 2016

<u>*Contemporary Romance Series*</u>

MacLarens of Fire Mountain

Second Summer, Book One
Hard Landing, Book Two
One More Day, Book Three
All Your Nights, Book Four
Always Love You, Book Five
Hearts Don't Lie, Book Six
No Getting Over You, Book Seven
'Til the Sun Comes Up, Book Eight, Releasing 2016

Peregrine Bay

Reclaiming Love, Book One, A Novella
Our Kind of Love, Book Two

The best way to stay in touch is to subscribe to my newsletter. Go to *www.shirleendavies.com* and subscribe in the box at the top of the right column that asks for your email. You'll be notified of new books before they are released, have chances to win great prizes, and receive other subscriber-only specials.

I care about quality, so if you find something in error, please contact me via email at shirleen@shirleendavies.com.

Description

Our Kind of Love – Book Two, Peregrine Bay Contemporary Romance Series

Selena Kerrigan is content with a life filled with work and family, never feeling the need to take a chance on a relationship—until she steps into a social world inhabited by a man with dark hair and penetrating blue eyes. Eyes that are fixed on her.

Lincoln Caldwell is a man satisfied with his life. Transitioning from an enviable career as a Navy SEAL to becoming a successful entrepreneur, his days focus on growing his security firm, spending his nights with whomever he chooses. Committing to one woman isn't on the horizon—until a captivating woman with caramel eyes sends his personal life into a tailspin.

Believing her identity remains a secret, Selena returns to work, ready to forget about running away from the bed she never should have gone near. She's prepared to put the colossal error, as well as the man she'll never see again, behind her.

Too bad the object of her lapse in judgment doesn't feel the same.

Linc is good at tracking his targets, and Selena is now at the top of his list. It's amazing how a pair of sandals and only a first name can say so much.

As he pursues the woman he can't rid from his mind, a series of cyber-attacks hit his business, threatening its hard-won success. Worse, and unbeknownst to most, Linc harbors a secret—one with the potential to alter his life, along with those he's close to, in ways he could never imagine.

Our Kind of Love, Book Two in the Peregrine Bay Contemporary Romance series, is a full-length novel with an HEA and no cliffhanger.

From the Author

Join Shirleen Davies' newsletter to receive notice of:
- New Releases
- Contests
- Free Reads and Sneak Peeks

To sign up, copy and paste this site address into your browser's address bar: http://bit.ly/1KqhKwm

Visit my website for a list of characters for each series.
http://www.shirleendavies.com/character-list.html

Acknowledgements

A special thank you to all those who have served our country in one of the military branches—Navy, Air Force, Army, Marines, and the United States Coast Guard. I am honored to count many of you as friends.

As always, many thanks to my wonderful resources, including my editor, Kim Young, proofreader, Alicia Carmical, Diane Lebow, who is a whiz at guiding my social media endeavors, my cover designer, Kim Killion, and Joseph Murray, who is a genius at formatting my books for both print and electronic versions.

Our Kind

Of Love

Prologue

Boise, Idaho
College Graduation

"What are your plans tonight, Selena?"

Selena Kerrigan turned to see the one man on campus she most wanted to notice her, Chad Donovan. The butterflies in her stomach went on high alert, buzzing around, creating chaos within her otherwise ordered life.

"My family will be leaving after dinner. I hadn't planned anything afterwards."

"Great. You can spend it with me and some of my friends. We'll be at the Mountain Top Inn before heading over to a friend's. I'll meet you at the restaurant." Chad turned and strode away without another word, leaving her confused and excited at the same time.

Dinner with her parents and sisters, Julia, Calypso, Danielle, and Lily, passed at a slow pace, her mind preoccupied with the upcoming party. The past four years had sped by with little time for social activities. Shy by nature, she'd accepted few dates, preferring to concentrate on her studies in preparation for her return to Peregrine Bay and a position in her family's real estate business.

Even the dates she did have turned out to be tiresome, listening to young men talk about themselves and future plans, then requiring her to respond. She'd never liked talking about herself. In her mind, she'd done little. Reading, old movies, fishing, hiking, and the occasional visit to the gym occupied her days. Besides having visited most of the fifty states, her family took a vacation to Europe each year. In her humble opinion, she'd seen much but done little, at least not enough to interest others.

Tonight, she'd be with someone who'd fascinated her since they first met her junior year. Handsome, gregarious, and popular, he'd always been polite yet oblivious to her—until he'd extended his invitation today.

"Are you all right?" Julia Kerrigan, Selena's older sister, sat next to her.

She hadn't confided in anyone about the party, not wanting to dampen the family's time together. Besides, her father wouldn't approve of her going off to some gathering without a proper escort. In his mind, she'd always be in need of his constant direction and guidance. She leaned toward her sister, keeping her voice low.

"I've been invited to meet someone later tonight and I'm a bit nervous."

Julia raised her eyebrows, turning her face toward Selena. "A date?"

"No, not exactly. Some people are meeting at a restaurant, then going to a friend's house." Her hands fidgeted in her lap, her eyes darting nervously between her stepmother and father.

"Do you know any of them?"

"Of course," she hedged. "Well…at least one. We've been in a couple classes together. I'd always hoped he would notice me, ask me out, but it never happened. This afternoon, he asked me to meet him at the restaurant."

"Maybe I should go with you—"

"No," Selena hissed, cutting Julia off. "I have to do this alone, and I don't want father and Joannie to know." Her father had been married three times. She and Julia had the same mother, Calypso another, and the twins, Danielle and Lily, another—their father's current wife, Joannie. Calypso attended college, and the twins were still in high school.

"All right, if you're sure. Here…" Julia rifled through her purse, handing Selena a card with the hotel and room number where she was staying. "I'm at a different hotel than father and I have my car. Call me if you need me."

She slipped the card into her purse, knowing it wouldn't be needed.

The moment dinner ended and her family drove away, Selena hopped into her car and took off for the Mountain Top Inn. It took about five minutes to locate Chad standing at the bar. As always, his friends, and those who wanted to be his friend, surrounded him, everyone talking at once. Walking towards him, she waved over the crowd, getting a wink in return, noticing the curious looks of those near Chad. No one else looked familiar.

"Hey, Selena. Glad you could make it. What do you want to drink?" Chad asked, taking her arm and pulling her toward him.

She didn't drink much, but wine always seemed safe. "Wine, please."

A minute later, she held a glass brimming with a healthy pour of white wine.

Chad placed a hand on her shoulder, leaning down so she could hear him over the noise. "We'll be leaving for the party in a few minutes. You may want to drink up."

She nodded and took a few sips, leaving the glass on the bar as he clasped her hand and walked toward the parking lot.

"You'll want to take your car. Is that all right?" he asked.

"I'd planned to take it."

"Great. Follow me."

It took twenty minutes to reach the turnoff, then another five to find a parking place. She locked her purse in the car, slipping her keys in a pocket, and looked around. Chad waited at the bottom of the stairs, motioning her toward him.

"Have you been here before?" he asked, taking her hand and leading her inside.

"Never."

He laughed, although she had no idea why, and headed toward a table filled with bottles of hard liquor, wine, and glasses. A tub filled with bottles of beer took up one end and a case of untouched water sat at the other. Chad poured her wine, then whiskey and cola for himself.

"Here you go. I need to speak with some friends. Take a look around, introduce yourself."

Selena lifted her face to reply, but he'd already left, disappearing into the crowd. She looked around, stunned at the number of people crammed into each of the main rooms. Laughter and the occasional shout pierced the air as she tried to spot even one person she recognized. Just like at the bar, there were no familiar faces.

Thirty minutes passed as she roamed the lower rooms, at one point taking a seat to watch the happenings. Occasionally, someone would introduce themselves, then move on.

As time passed, the noise level increased, the sounds of friendly laughter replaced with drunken shouts. She noticed people pairing off, some removing clothes and tossing them aside, oblivious to the others in the room. Most didn't seem to care about the display of partially clothed bodies, but Selena had no use for it.

After an hour, her empty glass her only companion, she decided to look for Chad and tell him she'd be leaving. She'd had enough of his party and his hospitality.

Standing, she reached out to steady herself, feeling lightheaded.

"Hey, you all right?" A strong hand gripped her elbow.

"Fine." Touching a hand to her forehead, Selena felt her cheeks flush. "I'm looking for Chad."

"Donovan?" the guy chuckled. "He'll be in one of the rooms upstairs. I'm sure he'd love to have you join him."

His slow perusal of her as he spoke triggered a queasy feeling in her stomach, accompanied by an inexplicable urge to run. First, she'd perform her social duty and inform Chad.

Selena took the stairs, then opened the door to the first room, finding two couples in various stages of undress, creating a mixture of laughter and moans. Shutting the door, she tried the next one, finding two women and a man on the bed, others standing around or leaning against the walls, staring, no one paying the slightest bit of attention to her. Selena's stomach churned as she backed out of the room.

One room remained. She grasped the handle, then stopped, deciding it may be best to leave and forget all about Chad and his party. The door opened as she began to turn away.

"Go on in. They won't mind." A girl of no more than sixteen giggled and walked out wearing nothing except a thin lace bra and panties.

Following the girl's retreat, Selena shook her head and turned to look through the open door. What she saw caused her breath to seize and jaw to drop.

The room was dark, except for floor-mounted lights aimed at the bed. Her gaze followed the light to see a woman on her hands and knees, Chad behind her, both naked. Two cameras filmed the scene, one person providing direction for the action. She tried to back away, but her feet remained frozen in place. She'd never seen anything like it.

The woman's loud moan pulled her from the trance. Her hand flew to her stomach, trying to quell the growing need to purge everything from her system. She stumbled down the hall and into a bathroom, kicking the door closed, falling in front of the toilet just as her stomach began to empty.

She didn't know how long she sat there, ignoring the occasional pounding or shouts from those who wanted access. Her head throbbed, but at least the rest of her felt numb. Selena had never thought herself a prude. She'd been to parties where porn movies played in private rooms. Although she'd never watched, neither their availability nor popularity bothered her. It wasn't her business what others wanted to watch.

Tonight, the unexpected display stunned her. Worse, the man who'd invited her to the party, the same man with whom she'd been longing to spend time with, was the star.

Pushing up from the floor, she brushed hair away from her eyes, then washed her face, feeling cold and clammy all at once. Drawing the door open, she peered into the hall, saying a prayer no one would notice her leaving.

It took a while for her to navigate her way home, but by two in the morning, she fell into bed, covering her face with both hands, vowing never to get caught in a situation like that again.

Chapter One

Peregrine Bay, Idaho
Seven years later

Selena groaned. She'd never expected Calypso to push her to honor the silly bet they'd made at Julia and Adam's wedding the week before. She and her four sisters had been sitting around, enjoying the reception, when Caly threw out a challenge. One Selena had been foolish enough to accept.

Calypso had joked about Selena's lack of dates and fear of going out. The conversation progressed until Selena had been defined by two words—boring and coward. Within minutes, Caly dared her to attend a party at some prominent citizen's house at the north end of Lake Bountiful. It was to celebrate the end of summer, and damned if she hadn't accepted—and she couldn't even blame alcohol.

She stood in front of the mirror, picking up one outfit after another, tossing each aside. None of them looked right. Her preference was to wear something flowing and lightweight, but the Idaho temperature had already begun to drop and evenings could turn chilly, especially by the lake. She sorted through her closet once more, hoping to find something suitable, when the doorbell rang and the front door squeaked open.

"Selena, it's Caly!"

"I'm in my bedroom." She lifted an armful of clothes from the closet and laid them on the bed.

"You ready to go?" Caly put her hands on her hips, spotting the clothes and her sister standing in nothing but her underwear. Lifting one brow, she grinned. "Hmm…guess not. How can I help?"

******

Within an hour, Selena sat behind the wheel of her car, following Caly to the party north of Pine Cove. Caly had been a gem, somehow pairing slacks with a blouse and sandals Selena never would've thought worked together. But then again, her sister always did have a flair for fashion.

Over the past week, Selena had done a little checking, discovering the host of the party owned a thriving security business and had graduated from the United States Naval Academy. One page listed him as a contributor to several charity organizations and a driving force behind revitalizing the area around the lake. Although it wasn't much, at least she felt equipped to make small talk if she ever met the man.

A sign up ahead pointed to a parking area. A shuttle van had been hired to take guests from their cars to the house, then back afterwards. She and Caly parked their cars, then boarded the van, her sister pointing to another sign saying the driver had the option to call a cab for anyone who'd partied too much. Selena was impressed.

She took a window seat, watching as the van climbed above the lake, then back down, following a private road lined on both sides with dense stands of western hemlock, white pine, and red cedar. Driving through an open gate supported by thick stone walls, her jaw dropped. To say the house was breathtaking would be an understatement.

Guests stepped off the bus and through twelve-foot-high double doors into a two-story entry with wide, curving staircases on both sides. Straight ahead stood a wall of glass with an unobstructed view of Lake Bountiful. Between the entry and glass lay a broad expanse of wood floors, hand-woven rugs, leather furniture—and at least two hundred people. So far, no one had appeared to greet them, which didn't seem to faze the other guests as they walked straight to the bar.

"Shall we?" Caly asked, slipping her arm through Selena's. "Let's get a drink, then find the host."

"Have you ever met him?"

"Never, but I have a description from the friend who tipped me off about the party. Come on."

As they waited in the drink line, Caly focused on a group of men a few feet away while Selena took in the room and view. To the left of the main house, another building stood near the lake. Built on pilings over the water, it also swarmed with people. Boats lined two docks, and it appeared a water taxi ferried guests from across the lake.

"What do you want?" Caly asked.

Selena hadn't even noticed they'd made it to the front of the line. "Uh…soda?"

"Oh no you don't. You're having a real drink. Either you pick something or I will."

She thought a moment, then smiled. "A dry martini with lots of olives."

Caly's brows lifted, the corners of her mouth tilting upward as she turned and ordered one for each of them.

Drinks in hand, they started winding a path into another room, which appeared to be an office or library, then out onto the expansive back deck where a band played a combination of rock, country, and blues. A few people danced, but most stood in small circles, talking and laughing. After an hour, they still had not seen their host, no one seeming the least concerned he hadn't appeared.

"May I get you another drink, ma'am?" A waiter stood next to Selena, reaching for her empty glass.

"We'll both have another dry martini with olives," Caly cut in, smiling at the young man.

Fresh drinks in hand, Caly became determined to locate their mysterious host, identifying eligible men for Selena at the same time.

"Caly, is that you?"

At the sound of the masculine voice, they glanced toward the band, both breaking out into wide grins.

"Devlin!" Caly jumped into their cousin's arms. He grunted, taking a step back at the impact.

"Whoa, sweetheart. I'm strong, but that's a robust frontal assault," he laughed, setting Caly down and offering a warm hug to Selena. "I didn't know you two would be here."

"I heard about it a couple weeks ago. Do you know the owner?" Caly asked.

"Nope. I came with a friend, who heard about it from someone else." He pointed toward a stunning redhead talking with a group of women near the band. "How did she get you to come along, Selena?"

"You must be the only Kerrigan unaware of the bet," Selena muttered.

"What bet?" He looked between the two. As part of the Lake Bountiful Hotshots, he'd been deployed fighting fires across most of the western United States, missing several family gatherings, including Julia and Adam's wedding.

"I bet Selena she wouldn't have the guts to attend this party." She glanced at her sister, who stared at her with a bland expression. "You know how much she loves parties…and drinking," she smirked.

Devlin knew he might be the only member of the family Selena had spoken to about her experience graduation night, leading to her subsequent discomfort of large parties and alcohol-induced fun. Over the years, she'd begun drinking an occasional cocktail, soda remaining her drink of choice.

"What do you have there, Selena?" He nodded toward her glass.

"A martini."

"Her second one," Caly added, as if it were some triumph on her part.

"Take it easy, sweetheart. Those will creep up on you without much warning." He finished his beer, watching her with narrowed eyes, knowing two should be her absolute limit. "I'm grabbing another beer. How about a soda?"

"One more martini for me, Dev," Caly answered.

"A soda for me would be great. Whatever they have." Selena looked at her glass, deciding she'd finish the martini before switching to the soda.

"I'll be right back." Dev lost himself in the crowd, which continued to grow, leaving little space indoors or out.

"Well, out of all these people, I wonder who our host is." Caly scanned the area, her nose twitching as the mystery deepened.

"Oh no…" Selena's voice trailed off as she raised her hand to her face. "I feel tingly."

Caly took the glass from her hand, set it on a nearby table, then helped Selena to a chair.

"You'd better sit for a while. I'll get you some water while Dev gets the soda. And no more alcohol for you."

Selena dragged her gaze from Caly's retreating back, feeling a little dizzy. After a few minutes she stood. Feeling much better, she decided to surprise Caly by locating their mysterious host. She put a hand over her mouth to stifle a giggle. *Yes, that's what I'll do. Surprise Caly*, she thought, disappearing into the large crowd.

She found herself standing at the bar, placing one hand on the edge to steady herself.

"Would you care for a drink?" the bartender asked.

She placed a finger to her lips, as if trying to make a decision. "Yes, I believe I will have a martini—dry with olives."

"Here you are." He watched her take the drink, wobbling slightly before steadying herself. "You going to be okay?"

"Oh, yes. I'm going to be great." She smiled, took a sip, then walked across the grass, not realizing the bartender had alerted someone in the crowd to keep an eye on her.

She found herself drawn to a group of men and women about her age who were deep in conversation. Finding her courage, Selena stopped next to them, listening as they spoke of the price of land and homes around the lake, a topic in which she was an expert.

"There is nothing affordable around the lake, except some piece of trash place across the road from the water." A bearded man, his arm around one of the women, finished his beer, pitching the empty into a nearby trash bin. "We're still looking, but it's bleak."

"Same here," another man said. "You have to be a millionaire like Linc to afford anything."

"Not necessarily." She couldn't believe she'd said the words out loud.

One of the men in the circle turned toward her. "Excuse me? Have we met?" His eyes crinkled with humor.

Selena cleared her throat. "I don't believe we have. So far, I've only seen two people I know, and I'm pretty certain you aren't one of them." She wobbled, then righted herself, hoping no one noticed.

Several in the group laughed, including the man next to her. He held out his hand. "I'm Linc. And you are?"

"Selena."

"It's good meet you, Selena. I believe you made a comment about the real estate market. Care to continue?"

She looked up, blinking a couple times before focusing on the man in front of her. The first thing she noticed was his height. He had to be a couple inches over six feet. The second thing were his piercing blue eyes, which seemed to bore into hers.

"Selena?"

"Hmm…what?"

He chuckled, holding out his hand to steady her as she leaned toward him. "The real estate market?"

"Oh yes. If memory serves, there are at least five homes on the lake considered affordable." She took another sip of her martini, feeling more light-headed by the second.

"And you would know that how?" Linc asked.

"I saw the listings, silly," she giggled. "How else would I know? Anyway, they're near Peregrine Bay." She looked around the group, her head bobbing. "That's at the other end of the lake." She closed her eyes, as if trying to remember how each listing read. "Let's see…one is on Eagle Way. Two bedrooms, two baths, boat dock. Another is off White Pine Road. Three bedrooms with boat dock." She took another sip, grimaced, and shook her head. "I think I'd better sit down."

Linc turned to the others. "I'll be back in a few," he said, his hand reaching out to steady her once again. "Come on, sweetheart. Let's find a place for you to sit down."

Selena looked up at him, her eyes bright. "That's what my cousin calls me. Sweetheart. I always like it when he says that." She pursed her lips, thinking. "Is it common?"

"What?" Linc asked, intrigued by the woman he guided toward the far end of the yard and up a few steps to a door leading into the house.

"A man calling a woman he barely knows sweetheart. Is it common?"

He chuckled, opening the door to his bedroom and helping her inside. "Yes, along with a few other terms. Come on. You can lay down here for a while to sleep it off." He helped her sit on the side of a bed.

"I think that's a very good idea."

"Good girl. I'll check on you in a little bit."

"Oh, that would be nice. Checking on me, I mean." She let out a sigh as her body slumped onto the bed.

Linc grabbed a blanket, laying it over her, noting she'd already passed out. He reached toward her, swiping an errant strand of hair from her face, drawing a finger down her cheek. Sitting down next to her, he watched as her breathing became deep and even. The longer he stayed, the more he wondered about her and how she'd come to be at his party.

Who are you, Selena? Do you belong to anyone? he asked himself as he watched her chest rise and fall.

She sighed again, rolling to her side, pulling the blanket with her.

Linc took a deep breath, placed his hands on his knees, and pushed himself up. He strolled to the door and took one last look behind him, certain she'd be gone when he returned.

Chapter Two

Selena opened her eyes, noting it was still dark, then reached toward her nightstand to grab the clock. Not finding it, she pushed herself up, gripping her head with both hands to still the pounding.

She thought of lying back down when the distinct sound of deep breathing, then a soft snore came from behind her. Her movement stilled, as did her breath. Trying to clear her head, she slowly turned, spotting the large form of a man a few inches away. Pulling the covers back, she looked down in horror to see she wore nothing except a cotton t-shirt and panties.

Her hands shook and her head pounded as she slipped from the bed, trying not to wake him. Selena used the moonlight seeping through an open window to find her clothes, then dashed into the bathroom. She closed the door and dressed, confirming her keys were still in a pocket. Opening the medicine cabinet, she grabbed a bottle of pain killers and downed two of them. Taking a deep breath, she turned the doorknob and peeked into the bedroom. He still slept.

Searching for her sandals, Selena glanced around, getting on her hands and knees to look under the bed. No luck. As the man turned toward her, moaning, she forgot the sandals, deciding to go barefoot. First, she wanted to take a good look at the man in the bed.

Trying her best to be quiet, Selena walked the few paces to the bed, leaned over, and stared. She had a vague recollection of him, but nothing more. Placing a hand on her heart, trying to still the beating threatening to burst through her chest, Selena came to the only conclusion she could— she'd slept with a man she didn't know and couldn't recall any of it.

Slow, quiet steps took her out of his room, through a hall, and to the entry doors. Seeing no one, Selena slipped outside, hit the lock button on the number pad, and ran. She kept going to the end of the asphalt drive and stopped. A tall metal gate protected the entrance from intruders, but she wondered if it also kept visitors inside. She searched for a keypad, anything that would allow her to open the hinged monster and take off. Pacing back and forth several times, looking around bushes and boulders, she found nothing. Looking toward the water, she spotted a place where the thick rock fortress sloped with the hillside, transitioning to a wooden fence. She followed it, wincing as branches scraped the bottom of her feet, but it was worth it. The ground had given way at one point, sinking to a foot below the bottom of the fence. It appeared to be just big enough for her to slide under.

She took one look at her party attire and shrugged, telling herself she had no other choice. A few minutes later, she stood on the other side and climbed back up the hill to the edge of the road, remembering the shuttle and long drive from the parking area.

Glancing toward the house one last time, she took a couple tentative steps onto the gravel road, found her courage, and began to run. The gravel stung her bare feet, slowing her down even when she stuck close to the dirt shoulder. All she had to do was focus on the road ahead, continue to move, and she'd be at her car in no time.

******

Linc's eyes opened to slits at the soft sound of movement somewhere in the house. The faintest amount of sunlight over the eastern mountains signaled daybreak. A groan escaped as he shot up and looked around to see no one else shared his bed. He looked toward the chair where he'd placed her clothes. Empty. Selena had gone.

He scrubbed a hand over his stubbled face, then ran it through his thick, dark brown hair, wondering how he'd slept through her departure. He must be getting old. A few years ago, while he'd still been an active member of the Navy SEALs, no one would've snuck away from him. One small movement would have him on alert, grabbing a weapon and taking action. No longer.

An injury during a successful extraction mission had set him back. He thought a little time in the hospital, a short recovery period, and he'd be back with his team. It hadn't happened that way. The injuries turned out to be more serious than anyone anticipated, resulting in impairment to his hearing and lung capacity—absolute requirements to continue as an active SEAL. One setback led to another, until his superiors gave him no other choice but to exit out with a medical disability. He'd been in his late twenties.

The sound of his phone had him scrambling for his clothes.

"Caldwell." He held the phone between his shoulder and ear as he slipped into his jeans, listening to the catering supervisor from his party. "No problem. Come on over."

Linc tossed the phone on the bed, deciding it best to take a quick check around the house to make sure no stragglers had been left behind. And if they had, that they wore enough clothes so as not to scare the caterer's clean-up crew.

He turned back toward the bed to grab his ringing phone.

"Boss, we have a problem."

"What is it?" Linc paced to the window, searching the back yard as if for intruders.

"A lone female just ducked under the fence and is heading toward the parking area by the main road. What do you want me to do?"

A grin tilted the corners of Linc's mouth, imagining his guest scrambling to get away.

"Nothing. Let her go."

"But—"

"She's harmless. I'm assuming there is still at least one car parked there, right?"

"Just one."

Linc almost chuckled. "Thanks for the call. We'll talk later about improving party security. Right now, I need to walk through the house."

He checked his office, family room, and garden room on his way to the kitchen for coffee before heading upstairs. Matt, a close friend, was out cold in one room, an arm wrapped around a woman with long blonde hair. He closed the door and headed for the next room, finding Shane, another buddy, cuddled up with his current girlfriend. The last two bedrooms were empty, as was the upstairs study. On a whim, he checked the bathrooms, hoping he wouldn't find someone passed out in the shower, which happened at his last party. He blew out a sigh of relief, finding them empty.

Ten minutes later, he stepped out of the shower, a towel wrapped around his waist, then shrugged into a clean t-shirt. Grabbing a pair of clean, well-worn jeans, he slipped into them, then sat on the bed, using the towel to dry the last drops of water from his hair. Bending down to shake it out, he spotted something shiny under the chair where he'd laid Selena's clothes. He reached underneath, grabbed the straps, and pulled out a pair of turquoise sandals. Smiling, he lifted them in front of him, knowing his guest had traveled to her car barefoot, and also understanding something else.

He now had two clues to his mystery woman. A first name and a pair of sandals. He'd tracked people with less.

******

"Pick up. Pick up." Caly paced, chanting into the phone on her third attempt to reach Selena. Around midnight, after searching for Selena and being told by a friend of the host she'd left the party an hour earlier, Caly had taken off. Their cousin, Devlin, had already left, citing plans to get up early for rock climbing with a group of his team members.

Caly left another message, debating whether or not to call Julia. She took a deep breath, reminding herself of the early hour. She'd give Selena a little more time to return her messages before calling Julia. She poured more coffee, lifting the cup to her lips when the phone rang.

She grabbed it. "Selena?"

"Yes, it's me."

"Where the hell have you been? I've called three times."

"Sorry to worry you, but I just got home."

"You're just now getting home?" Caly would've smiled if her sister's voice hadn't sounded so distraught.

"Look, I'll explain it all later. Right now, I need to lay down before my head splits open." Selena punched the speakerphone button and set it on a table. "What do you do for a hangover?"

"Three things—drink lots of orange juice, take a hot shower, and go to bed," Caly replied, stifling a chuckle. "Oh, and don't drink coffee or anything with caffeine. Juices and water, or a virgin Bloody Mary with a stick of celery. Have you taken any pain killers?"

"Yes, but they don't seem to be helping." Selena pressed the palms of her hands against her eyes, hoping the pressure would relieve the pain. "I'm going to get in the shower. I'll talk to you later."

"Get some rest because I'm coming over tonight and you're going to tell me everything that happened last night."

Selena groaned. It would be a short conversation. She had no idea what she'd done last night or with whom she'd done it.

Finishing two glasses of orange juice, she stepped into the shower and let the hot water sluice down her neck and back, feeling much of the tension ease away, even though it did little for the thundering in her head. Wrapping herself in a full body towel, she pulled a comb through her hair before her energy gave out. She lowered herself onto the bed, thinking of the man she'd shared a bed with…and maybe more.

In sleep, except for the dark stubble on his jaw and chin, he looked to be in his mid-twenties. She recalled his features seemed somewhat familiar. If she'd taken more time, perhaps her memory would have returned, helping her remember his name, or at least something about him.

She turned onto her back, covering her face with both hands, embarrassment causing a flush to creep up her neck and cheeks. Maybe sleep would help, although she doubted it. The truth was she'd gotten drunk, allowed herself to be picked up by some stranger, and ended up in his bed. She would've considered that more, except the heaviness of her eyelids won out over thought and she drifted into a deep sleep.

Chapter Three

"I still think turning off most of the security for your party was a bad decision." Matt Tarantino, Linc's best friend, partner, and Vice President of Operations at Templar Security & Rescue, downed his second cup of coffee as the sun rose over the mountains to the east.

The company was comprised of two divisions. One offered high-level security for wealthy individuals and high-profile clients. The second offered rescue and extraction services for adventurers or those working in high-risk locations. Attracting type-A personalities, adventure travel had become a booming business for vacationers choosing to spend their off-time participating in dangerous activities.

The daily meetings included Linc, Matt, and Shane Gardner, his other close friend and Vice President of Client Acquisition, a fancy name for sales, for both divisions. Linc founded the company and held the majority share of stock. Matt and Shane owned minority interests, although Linc considered them partners in all ways that mattered.

They began at six each morning, discussing extraction operations and security issues, such as today when Matt wanted to discuss the last minute decision to curtail much of the security that protected Linc at his home. Linc had overridden Matt's recommendation to keep all security operational.

"Is this about my decision to minimize security last night, or did something happen during the party?"

Matt shook his head. "Except for the woman who left your bed at dawn, there were no breaches."

"*Ran* from my bed is more accurate." Linc chuckled, thinking of the sandals sitting on the dresser in his bedroom.

Matt and Shane shared a look. They'd never known Linc to have women stay over at his house. He'd always had a firm policy of staying at their place, never opening his bedroom to any female, no matter how long they'd been together.

"So what's the issue?" Linc directed his question to Matt.

"The party was by open invitation. Anyone could attend, including those who have an ax to grind with either you or TSR. We had no one stationed at the gate or front door to check for weapons or identification. Anyone with basic security knowledge could have used the party as an opportunity to scope out your system, figuring out how to disable it."

"We've gone over this before, Matt. I know you're concerned about any breach to my system becoming a public relations nightmare."

"I *am* concerned. Competition is fierce and getting tougher all the time. Anyone with military experience believes they can open a security firm, using any situation to their advantage, including disabling the personal residence of TSR's president." Matt sat forward, resting his arms on the table. "I think we need to go about it in a different way for any future parties."

Linc narrowed his gaze at Matt. Perhaps he had gone too far in trying to make guests feel welcome and comfortable. He shifted toward Shane. "What are your thoughts?"

"I agree with Matt. We shouldn't have disabled the systems. What was the point? I assume you had one, and I'd like to hear what it was." Shane crossed his arms and leaned back, his face impassive.

Shane was right. Linc did have a reason for deactivating the security for one night.

He stood, walking to the counter to fill his coffee cup, then topping off Matt's and Shane's.

"I held the party for one reason only—to give our neighbors a chance to get to know the three of us and other members of TSR. We've lived in secrecy too long, causing rumors to circulate that can be damaging to our expansion plans. By opening the doors without heightened security, which might have discouraged attendance, guests got to see we are no different from them. Three men working hard to grow a company while offering the finest security and rescue services available. I believe it was a good decision." He shot a knowing look at Matt. "I noticed you got pretty close to one of the guests."

"Yeah, my good fortune." Matt grinned. "She was in the group when we discussed real estate prices and your somewhat intoxicated bedmate joined us."

"Hell, the woman was drunk on her ass. She passed out cold as soon as she hit my bed."

"Guess you got to play babysitter, and in your own bedroom, too. A new role for you, huh?" Shane snorted.

Linc glared at his friends. "If we're finished discussing the party, let's focus on the main subject of the meeting—a new security system for the arts center in Peregrine Bay."

"We're on the short list with three other firms." Shane pulled out some papers, handing copies to both men. "This is their final criteria for making a decision."

"Tell us about the competition." Linc scanned the information, then looked at Shane.

Shane ticked off the names of one headquartered in Seattle, another in Portland, and one in Salt Lake City, all run by ex-military. "Simondson Security, the Portland firm, is the most aggressive. They're planning to open an office in Boise."

"And their tactics?" Linc asked, warming to the subject.

"As tough as you'd expect," Shane answered. "Last Wednesday, I fired the salesman we hired three weeks ago. Found out he was a mole for Simondson. He kept criticizing our techniques and systems, questioning everything. Our people became suspicious, so I put Brut on his tail. It took a few days, but we found out he's the cousin of Simondson himself. The good news is he completed a fraction of his training, not getting to the real high-level stuff."

Linc nodded, sitting back and crossing his arms. "Nothing I didn't expect at some point. What do we need to do to win the contract?"

"Word has it the Seattle firm will probably pass on providing a bid. They just received an award for work in Bellingham and are tapped out. Salt Lake will need to scramble to find enough qualified techs to complete the work on time, which indicates they'll probably bid up to cover the costs. I believe Simondson is our major competition on this. I'll work the numbers so they get our best equipment at the lowest price. You'll need to pull out the famous Caldwell charm and focus it on three key people—Mayor Timmons, Councilman Tom Harten, who heads the search committee, and the chamber president, Julia Kerrigan Monroe."

Linc's head shot up. "Chief Monroe's wife?"

"That's the one. Don't you know him?"

"I do. Met Adam when he was a detective in Spokane handling a murder investigation involving one of our clients."

"The one where the perp said he broke through our security?" Matt asked.

"That's the one. Turned out he was already in the house, banging our client's wife. When the husband returned home, the whole situation got out of hand. When it was over, the wife's lover was dead. Monroe was in charge of the investigation. Good man."

"We installed the security system at Monroe's house," Matt added. "So I guess you'll be getting together with them."

"And the mayor. Not sure about Harten. From what I hear, the man's a loose cannon with a big mouth. His attitude pisses off a lot of people. I'm surprised he's on the award committee." Linc made notes as he talked, deciding he had some other business with Adam Monroe.

"His daddy is the one who donated the land for the arts center. Money talks…" Shane's voice drifted off as he slid the folder into his case and stood. "If there's nothing else, I have a meeting in thirty minutes. Let me know how you do with the people in Peregrine Bay."

******

"All right. I've waited two days. I expect you to cough up details. Now." Calypso walked straight to the cabinet in Selena's kitchen, grabbed a wine glass, and filled it with her favorite Malbec before glancing at her sister. "Aren't you drinking?" She raised an eyebrow.

Selena groaned, placing a hand over her stomach. "Probably never again. I don't know why people continue to drink when all they get is a hangover. Anyway, I have my cranberry juice." She tilted her glass toward Caly.

"Most people learn how much they can drink and stop before they get there. Your only problem was you didn't know your limit. Now you know."

"Yeah. None...zero." She settled onto a barstool. "And I'm not talking about the party, with you or anyone else. All I want to do is forget the entire night."

"I don't know why. You seemed to be having a great time until we got separated. Devlin looked everywhere for you. We both thought you'd left early." Caly placed a hand on Selena's shoulder. "I won't bug you to tell me anything. Whatever happened is your secret."

Selena nodded, wanting nothing more than to hide in her bedroom, pull the covers over her head, and let time pass until the nightmare went away. She didn't want to admit to anyone she had no memory of what happened, other than waking up almost naked in a stranger's bed. As much as she wanted to deny it, she had to assume they'd slept together. She buried her head in her hands and groaned.

"You all right?" Caly asked. She'd never seen Selena act like this, but she'd never seen her drunk or with a two-day hangover, either. Selena also never missed work, yet she had today.

"Other than this constant headache, I'm fine." She slid off the stool, heading for her bedroom. "Let yourself out whenever you're ready. I'm going back to bed."

Selena closed her door, then leaned against it, closing her eyes. Humiliation mixed with confusion had consumed her since waking up. Priding herself on being sensible and always in control, the feeling of vulnerability grated on her. The idea someone knew more about their night together than she did terrified her.

Grabbing a bottle from her dresser, she popped an over-the-counter sleep aid in her mouth, washing it down with a full glass of water. She'd sleep the rest of the day and all night. Tomorrow, she'd be her old self and vowed to forget she'd ever attended the party.

******

"Thanks for meeting with me, Adam. We missed you at the party." Linc shook his outstretched hand, taking a seat.

"Sorry about that. Julia and I had a failure of communication." Adam shoved papers aside. As the police chief of Peregrine Bay, he never seemed to have enough desk or file space for the mounds of paperwork. "I'm guessing you're not here to admire my pretty face."

Linc chuckled. "Not hardly. You probably know my company is bidding on providing the security system for the new arts center in town." He set the bid specs on Adam's desk.

"You know I'm not allow—"

Linc held up his hand. "I'm not looking for the inside track. What I *am* interested in is learning more about Councilman Tom Harten. He's one of the three individuals involved in making the final decision."

"Along with Julia and the mayor." Adam cocked his brow.

"I know they'll make the right decision for the town, and I can live with that. My concern lies with Harten. To be honest, I haven't heard anything good about the man."

Adam stood and closed the door, turning to face Linc. "He's a piece of work. I'd be interested to learn what you've heard."

"It's all hearsay. I don't know if it will do you much good."

"Let me decide if it's worthwhile or not." Returning to his desk, Adam took a seat, leaning forward.

"I trust this won't go beyond this room."

Adam nodded at Linc's request.

"Word is he's been the recipient of kickbacks, bribes, anything that will line his pockets. An honest bid process seems to be beyond him." Linc sat back, narrowing his gaze. "Tell me you haven't heard the same."

Adam's face remained impassive as he pondered Linc's accusations. It was nothing he hadn't heard before about their illustrious councilman.

"You've heard this from more than one source?"

Steepling his fingers under his chin, Linc nodded. "More than one. All reliable."

"My office is looking into similar allegations. I can't tell you specifics, but they've been building since before I took office. The problem is he's from a wealthy family with deep roots in Peregrine Bay."

"And his daddy has a lot of land to donate for city projects."

Adam's brows shot up. "How'd you hear that?"

"As I said, I've got very reliable sources."

"You know, they've added a couple people to the selection committee."

"When?" Linc asked.

"Yesterday. The leader of the arts council and Herman Jost, a businessman and supporter of the arts."

"Jost…the name sounds familiar."

"He owns a jewelry store." Adam smiled, remembering the conversations he'd had with the man since high school. "Getting on in years, but sharp as anyone, and honest. He's no fan of Tom Harten."

Linc stood, grabbing his file off the desk. "I'm just looking for an honest bid system. At least now I have a better sense of what I'm up against."

"You worried?"

"Hell no. We don't lose often and I don't intend to this time. Let me know if you're ever up my way. I'll meet you for a beer."

"Done."

Linc reached for the doorknob, then turned back. "Another question. Do you happen to know a woman with wheat-colored hair, warm brown eyes, slender…" His voice trailed off when Adam chuckled. "What?"

"That could describe several women in town. Do you have a name?"

"Just a first name. Selena. I think she might be involved in real estate."

Adam's smile faded at the mention of his sister-in-law. "Selena Kerrigan."

"Julia's sister?"

"The same." Adam took a few steps closer. "Why?"

Linc didn't miss the warning on Adam's face. "She was a guest at my party. Left something behind I'd like to return to her. Does she work at Kerrigan Real Estate?"

"She does. Why don't you give it to me? I'll see that she gets it."

"It's no problem. Besides, it's in the car. I'll drop it off on my way north. Thanks again."

Adam shook his head. He had nothing but respect for Linc and his accomplishments. At least the ones involving business. Although they'd known each other for years, he knew almost nothing about the man's personal life, other than being ex-military and single. As with most active and former Navy SEALs, Adam had always suspected Linc had no problem finding female companionship. He just hoped Selena wasn't his next target.

Chapter Four

"Glad to see you're feeling better, Selena. We were worried about you." Tricia, their office manager and mother hen, walked up, taking a good look at her. "You *are* feeling better, right?"

"Much better than yesterday." Selena glanced at her overflowing mail slot. "Guess I have some catching up to do."

"Can you imagine what it would be like if you ever took a vacation?" Tricia meant it as a joke, but the look on Selena's face told her she'd failed. "You know, it might be good for you to take some time off. You're here at least six days a week, sometimes seven. It's not healthy to work so much without taking a break to play."

"I have fun."

"When? Where? With whom?" Tricia had known all the Kerrigan girls since they were young, and met all three of Joshua Kerrigan's wives. It had torn the family apart when Julia and Selena's mother discovered Joshua's affair with Breeze, who'd become his second wife and Calypso's mother. When Breeze died, he raised the three girls alone until falling in love with Joannie, the twin's mother. Of all the daughters, Selena had always been the most serious, only attending social affairs as required by her family, dating little, and working much too hard.

"I, um…went to a party this past weekend. So, you see, I can have fun. Guess it's time for me to get to work."

"You know, the offer still stands to use our cabin up in the mountains if you ever want to get away," Tricia called after her. "Think about it."

Selena waved a hand in the air in acknowledgment, grateful for Tricia's friendship, then closed her office door. She needed to get to work, catch up on what she'd missed during her day in bed, and purge the party from her mind. It would be tougher to rid her thoughts of the man who'd slept beside her.

Letting out a breath, she pulled her chair closer to the desk and began to check email. After a while, the routine of being in the office, getting back to what she knew, began to pull her mind from her alcohol-induced bad judgment. Her muscles relaxed and her mood lightened as she searched for the perfect home for a new client. Before she knew it, two hours had passed without a thought of Saturday night. Sitting back, Selena checked the time, deciding lunch sounded good a moment before Tricia buzzed her.

"There's a potential client in the waiting area. Do you have time for a meeting or would you like me to schedule something?"

Considering it for a brief moment, she decided a new client took precedence over her stomach. "Now is fine." It took mere seconds before she heard a knock on her door. She stood.

"Come in."

Linc stepped into her office, dangling a pair of sandals from his fingers. "Cinderella, I presume." He shot her a wry smile, his gaze boring into hers, as Selena's face turned from curiosity to horror.

******

Stepping forward, taking a certain amount of enjoyment at watching her jaw drop, Linc extended his hand.

"Lincoln Caldwell. I don't believe we've been properly introduced."

Staring at the outstretched hand, her gaze wandered to the sandals dangling by his side, feeling her face heat. Clearing her throat, she stepped around the desk, taking his hand in hers.

"Mr. Caldwell." She wished for a witty retort, something to calm the butterflies in her stomach. Instead, she plastered a smile on her face. "I'm Selena Kerrigan, but I guess you already know that." Noticing his eyes crinkle in amusement, she felt his grip tighten on hers, triggering a spark of awareness. "I, uh…see you found my missing shoes." Dropping her hand, she took a step back, needing to calm her reaction to the man.

The image of him fast asleep in the large bed came rushing back. He'd looked boyishly handsome in the rumpled bed, his hair tousled, his face relaxed. The person standing before her was all man without a trace of the gentle image she'd seen in sleep.

He chuckled, seeing Selena gripping her hands together, trying to stop the slight tremor he'd noticed earlier. "It was hard to miss them, Ms. Kerrigan."

"Oh?"

"They were lying by my bed." He held the bright turquoise sandals aloft. "A little hard to overlook, don't you think?"

A low groan escaped before she reached out, snatching the shoes from his hand.

Touching the back of the chair, he nodded toward it. "Mind if I sit down?"

"Um…no. Please, take a seat. Can I get you water, coffee, a soda?" Her voice squeaked, signaling the uneasiness churning through her.

"Actually, if you haven't eaten, I'd like to take you to lunch. After all, we seem to have quite a bit in common."

She didn't need to look in a mirror to know her face had turned bright red.

"I don't think we need to discuss anything, Mr. Caldwell."

"Please. Call me Linc. I believe we know each other well enough for first names, don't you?"

Linc. The name brought back a vague recollection of the party, a group of people, and someone offering her help when the alcohol clouded her brain. Linc, the man she'd woken up next to.

She'd just begun to feel like herself when his comment triggered a blush starting at her toes and spreading through her body. Touching her forehead, she dropped her arm, taking a step toward him.

"Mr. Caldwell—"

"Linc."

"Fine. Linc. I'm not sure what you are referring to, but I do thank you for locating my property and returning it. Although, I'm not clear on how you figured out they were mine."

"You told me your name Saturday night. I happened to have a meeting with the police   chief—"

"Adam?" She groaned, her hand reaching out to the edge of her desk to steady herself.

"Your brother-in-law, I believe. I figured if anyone knew someone named Selena who worked in real estate, Adam would. Saved me a lot of time. Now, let me take you to lunch. You look like you could use a drink."

One hand flew to her mouth as the other grasped her stomach. Shaking her head, she dashed past him, running down the hall.

******

"Are you certain I can't get you a glass of wine?" Linc studied her, already figuring out Selena wasn't much of a drinker.

"No. Tea is fine. Thank you." Her hands grasped the glass in front of her as if it could shield her from the man sitting across the table. Hiding in the bathroom felt so silly, yet the moment he'd mentioned a drink, her stomach roiled and a cold sweat spread across her forehead. Splashing water on her face, she'd gained enough control to return to the office, hoping Linc had given up and left. He hadn't.

Instead, he'd picked up her purse, cupped her elbow, and escorted her outside without a backward glance at a slack-jawed Tricia. Selena knew she'd have a lot of explaining to do when she returned.

Shifting uncomfortably under his gaze, she picked up her glass, taking a long swallow before setting it on the table with a shaky hand. Looking around the room, several people nodded at her or waved. All she could muster was an uneasy smile. By afternoon, the entire town would know she had lunch with a handsome man. Some may even know his name.

Clenching a fork, she pushed her salad around on the plate, taking a small bite.

"Hello, Linc. I thought that was you sitting with Selena." Mayor Timmons grasped Linc's hand, then leaned down to place a kiss on Selena's cheek. "I didn't know you knew the Kerrigans."

"I can't say as I know any of them except Selena and Julia."

Selena's gaze shot to Linc's, her spine stiffening. This was worse than she thought. He'd spoken to Adam, who'd speak to his wife, and before she had a chance to form a response, Julia would be in her office, asking questions.

Linc looked back at her. "I had business in town and thought it a good time to catch up with her. Right, Selena?"

Her face took on a green tinge as she worked to maintain a weak smile. "Um…right."

"Well, I won't keep you. Just wanted to say hello. I'll see you at supper this weekend, Selena." The mayor turned toward the door, Linc following his exit. He then looked back at Selena.

"Supper?"

"He's a distant uncle by marriage. I've known him my entire life. He usually joins us at my father's home on Sunday afternoons." She stopped, realizing her rambling did nothing to bring their lunch to a swift end. Fixing her gaze on him, Selena leaned forward. "Is there a reason you wanted to have lunch with me?"

"How much do you remember about Saturday night?"

Her face paled as she sat back in her seat. Licking her lips, she struggled for a good answer, settling for the truth. Resting her hands on the table, she took a deep breath.

"Not much."

"I didn't think so." Reaching across the table, he settled his hand on hers. "You don't drink much, do you?"

"Was it so obvious?" Her face fell, but she didn't pull her hand away.

He would've chuckled if she didn't look so utterly miserable. Linc had always been good at figuring people out. Few women could get past his excellent instincts, although many had tried to play games or portray themselves as someone they weren't. Across the table sat a woman who seemed to have little experience being coy or concealing her feelings. Her apparent naiveté was intriguing and refreshing compared to the constant stream of women throwing themselves at him.

He lowered his voice, glancing around to make certain no one heard. "You have nothing to be embarrassed about,

Selena. I'm not here to make you believe anything happened between us."

Her eyes flashed in relief. "It didn't?"

"No." He leaned closer. "Not because I didn't want it to, but I make it a point never to take advantage of a woman who won't remember me the following day." His smile warmed her.

"That's good. Very good." Her brows drew together. "Wait. You *wanted* something to happen between us?"

He chuckled, squeezing her hand before letting go, feeling the loss of her touch in an instant. "I do try to be a gentleman, but I'm not dead. You're beautiful and genuine, from what I've seen, which is a rare quality. If you hadn't had your fill of martinis, I would've been tempted to see where the night would lead."

"Instead, I collapsed in your bed."

"Well, I think you collapsed several yards before that." Linc's eyes flickered as his mouth tilted up.

"This keeps getting worse and worse. I should've said no, never followed my sister to your place, and never ordered a martini. I don't know what got into me."

Tilting his head, he felt an unaccustomed surge of sympathy. He couldn't remember the last time anyone had elicited such compassion. He'd come from a hard-edged military family and had only one goal in mind—secure a slot at the Naval Academy. Graduating near the top of his class allowed him the opportunity to become a SEAL.

At the time, the BUD/S training had been the most grueling period in his life. Quitting, however, had never been an option. He'd made it through, including the advanced training, and thrived, loving every minute. Being forced to accept a medical discharge had changed his life. It had taken a long time to find pleasure as a civilian and his work. If not for the ongoing support of his SEAL team, plus his close friendship with Matt and Shane, he might still be rolling around in the hole he'd dug for himself.

"I take it you're not a partier."

Selena slapped a hand over her mouth at the unintended snort. "Not even close. If it hadn't been for a stupid bet I made with one of my sisters, I never would've been there. And you would never have had to track me down."

"Do you honestly believe I mind seeing you again?"

Her eyes widened, lips parting. "Don't you feel hunting for a woman who misplaced her shoes is a waste of time?" She wondered why he'd taken the time to track her down, doubting her appeal to a man who so obviously had no trouble with women.

Without answering, he glanced at the bill, tossed money on the table, then stood, walking to her chair and pulling it out.

"Come on. It's time to get out of here." Placing a hand on the small of her back, Linc guided her outside, turning the opposite direction of her office.

"Wait. My office is that way." She glanced over her shoulder toward the other end of town.

"I know."

Loving the feel of his hand on her back, she fought the urge to lean into him. Instead, she forced her attention straight ahead, nodding at a few people, smiling at others.

"Where are we going?" she asked as they crossed the street, moving away from the commercial district.

He glanced down at her, not slowing his pace. "I don't know Peregrine Bay well, but as I recall, there's a park up here with a great view of the water. I thought we'd continue our talk away from the prying ears of your friends."

Selena swallowed, hoping he expected a tour of downtown, or maybe directions to his next meeting. Continuing their talk didn't even rank as something she wanted to do. Squaring her shoulders, she continued to let him lead until he stopped at a bench not more than ten feet from the water's edge.

"This will work." Linc waited until she settled on the bench, then sat next to her, leaving mere inches between them.

"So, what is it you want to talk about?"

Chapter Five

Portland, Oregon

"Get me as much information as you can on TSR and the owner, Lincoln Caldwell. I want to know how the company started, his background, extracurricular activities, including who he's sleeping with, and anything else you can dig up on the guy." Greg Nelson looked up from the folder he'd been reviewing.

"Sure thing, boss." The company security officer walked toward the door.

"Also, find out what you can on Matt Tarantino and Shane Gardner. Same criteria as for Caldwell. One of them will have *something* in their past we can use as leverage." Greg scribbled a couple notes, then closed the folder as the man nodded and left the office. Winning the bid for the art center in Peregrine Bay would be a solid start for their new office in Idaho. They already had two projects for commercial work in his hometown of Boise. A third would identify them throughout the state as a major competitor.

Greg had left Boise after college, enlisting in the Army, becoming a member of the elite Special Forces. Retiring after twenty years, he'd accepted an offer with Simondson Security in Portland, taking over as president a few years later when the founder elevated himself to chairman. Greg had worked hard, almost losing a marriage in his quest to make it to the top in the crowded security field. He believed knowing more about his competitors than they knew about Simondson would increase the chances for success, even if you never used the information against anyone.

"Greg, Ephraim called. He's on his way in and wants to meet with you." The office manager shrugged, closing the door after her announcement.

Setting down his pen, Greg grabbed his cup and an additional one for the chairman of the company. Ephraim Simondson always had black coffee within easy reach when he held a meeting, especially an unannounced one. In his late sixties, the founder came to the office for a few hours three or four times a week, spending the rest of his time on business development or in board meetings for the many charitable organizations he supported. Greg figured Ephraim's reason for driving to the office a second time in one day must be important.

"Greg." Ephraim burst into the room, taking the cup Greg offered and sitting down. Short and wiry, he sported a trim physique honed from years of faithful workouts and the occasional marathon. He kept his graying hair cut short, military style, and he pulsed with energy at all times. "I have another meeting across town, but need to discuss an idea with you." He took a sip of coffee, then sat back. "My stepson is moving up to Boise. That's where he's from. He graduated from the state college. Now he's looking to break out of what he's doing and get a fresh start. I'd like you to find him a position."

Greg stifled a groan. He'd heard little about the stepson, although he knew Ephraim put up with him to please his wife, a woman twenty years younger. High-maintenance came to mind whenever Greg saw her.

"What type of position?" He didn't need any unqualified employees taking up space.

"Hell, I don't know. Errands, filing, meeting with potential clients. Yes, that might work. He's a good-looking kid and makes a decent impression."

Greg knew Ephraim used the word "kid" loosely, as his stepson had to be close to thirty. "Does he have sales experience, any background relevant to security?"

"No, but you're an excellent mentor. I'm certain you'll find the right spot for him." Standing, he set his cup down. "I'll get you more information tonight. He's due in Portland in a few days, then he'll fly to Boise by the end of the week. I'd appreciate it if you could set something up with him before he leaves." Without waiting for a response, Ephraim left in much the same fashion as he entered. Greg wondered if the man ever did anything at a normal speed.

Slapping his hands on the desk, Greg stood, deciding he'd talk to the man selected to run the Boise office. Between the two of them, they'd figure something out so Ephraim's stepson could be productive without negatively impacting the bottom line. After all, hiring him wasn't a request. It was an order.

******

Of all the requests Linc could have made as they watched the water lap up on shore, his desire for her to accompany him to an out-of-town high-profile fundraising event took Selena by surprise. She didn't know what to expect—an introduction to someone in local politics, a break on the commission for a future real estate deal, even a meeting with her father, a well-known developer—but definitely not a date. Well, not an actual *date*. She would act as a placeholder so he could attend the event in peace without being bombarded by single women with expectations.

"Why me? You must have many other choices with more to offer." She didn't care if her reaction sounded defensive. Anyone who knew her understood she wasn't the social person in the family. Calypso Kerrigan took the honor of being the preferred date of any man looking for a combination of beauty, brains, and bull without strings. Flashy, yet classy, she could stroll into a room, dance every dance, never buy a drink, and walk out with several requests for her phone number. Requests she turned down on a regular basis.

They'd walked to the edge of the lake, looking over the water as a hawk circled above, a group of ducks swimming near the pier. She loved this time of day and this part of the lake. Today, she hadn't been able to enjoy either.

"You're perfect. The fundraiser is in Spokane, not here. It's put on by the building association and local realtors.

You'll have no problem feeling comfortable and conversing intelligently. And my most important criteria, you'll expect nothing from me."

"And you know that how?" Even though the day had turned warm, she crossed her arms, rubbing her hands up and down to fend off the chill.

He chuckled as he removed his jacket, draping it around her shoulders.

"You already had the perfect opportunity when you crashed in my bed. When you woke, you couldn't get away from me fast enough. I can't think of another woman who's shared my bed and not wanted to make more of it than what it was."

Her brows shot up at his arrogance. She might not date much, and had little experience with men compared to his experience with women, but she could recognize a man with an overinflated belief in his attraction to the opposite sex. Except for one thing. Linc Caldwell had a presence few men could match.

At over six feet tall with piercing blue eyes that telegraphed nothing and deep brown hair with a hint of red, he made a striking figure. His erect stance indicated a man comfortable with himself and his abilities, someone who accepted no excuses and took no prisoners. He expected, and got, what he wanted, going after his goals with an intensity beyond most men. From what she'd heard, he worked hard to get to this point. She couldn't find fault with that.

Reaching out to tuck a strand of hair behind her ear, Linc brushed his fingers down her cheek before letting his hand drop away.

"We'll fly to Spokane, enjoy a fine dinner, and mingle. You'll have your own room at the hotel. If there's anything you'd like to see, we can stay the following day—make a weekend of it." He watched as one delicate brow arched. "Besides, I'd appreciate your company."

Selena drew in a ragged breath at the sincerity in his voice and eyes. If she were Calypso, she'd jump at the opportunity for a free trip to Spokane and an evening with someone as compelling as Linc.

"I don't believe I'm the best person for what you need. My sister, Caly, would be perfect. She thrives on social events such as the one you're attending. You'd be quite proud to have her on your arm for the evening."

He took a step forward, not sure why or what he wanted to say. Something about Selena touched him. Linc studied her face—the set of her beautiful mouth, the softness in her eyes, the earnestness in her voice.

"Believe me, I would be more than proud to have you on my arm, Selena. Besides, I don't believe you'd want others to know I have my own Cinderella."

Her nostrils flared as she moved away. "You wouldn't."

"Of course I would. It's not often a man has an encounter with such an intriguing apparition, then discovers she left something of herself behind." His eyes sparkled as a smile curved the corners of his mouth.

"That isn't fair. You're using my poor judgment against me. It's not gentlemanly or gracious in any way." The pitch of her voice increased with each word.

"Ah, Ms. Kerrigan. When did I ever say I was a gentleman or gracious. I'm a man who knows what he wants, and right now, I want you to accompany me to Spokane as my guest. If needed, I'll give you my word nothing will happen between us—unless you wish it, of course."

"That's preposterous. Of course I don't want anything to happen. My life is fine the way it is without some arrogant man who has an inflated sense of his appeal. Makes me wonder how in the world you have so many women standing in line for your attentions." She turned, walking away from him in the direction of her office.

Jogging to catch up, he leaned close to her. "But you'll do it. You'll travel to Spokane with me."

She let out an exasperated breath. "Yes, damn you. I'll do it," she hissed. Forcing a smile, she nodded at an elderly couple before turning back to him, steel in her voice. "Then I never want to see you again."

******

"Good afternoon, Tricia." Caly breezed into the office after a busy day showing property to potential renters. "Anything happening?"

"Nothing much, except Selena storming in a little while ago. I've never seen her so angry. Slammed her office door and I haven't seen her since."

Caly stared down the hall, lifting an eyebrow. "Any idea what's bothering her?"

Tricia handed Caly her mail, shrugging. "It was a pretty normal day until a potential client showed up. Seems the day went downhill from there."

"Did you write down the client's name?"

She glanced at her log to verify the name. "Linc Caldwell. Tall, a real looker, and no wedding ring." She looked up to see Caly dashing down the hall, throwing open Selena's door.

"Linc Caldwell was here? In your office?" Caly gasped, shutting the door behind her. "How did he find you?"

Selena closed the computer site she'd been searching, her shoulders slumping. "Yes, he was here, and it appears our dear brother-in-law told him."

Caly settled into a guest chair. "Adam? How in the world—"

"Linc had a meeting with him. He remembered my name and asked Adam if he knew a Selena involved in real estate. It wasn't Adam's fault."

"I don't understand why he wanted to see you. Did you two meet at the party?"

Selena leaned down, picked up her sandals, and held them in the air.

"You left your shoes at his house?"

"His bedroom, actually." Selena groaned, burying her face in her hands. She'd told Caly nothing about the particulars the night of the party, letting her assume she'd passed out on the host's sofa. It seemed pointless to hide anything now.

Caly's mouth opened, then closed, her eyes wide. "You told me you had too much to drink and passed out. Am I missing something, or did you spend the night with Linc? And I mean *with* him."

"I told you the truth. I simply omitted *where* I passed out." Picking up a bottle of water, she took her time unscrewing the cap and taking a long swallow. "I woke up in his bed. He was sound asleep, so I got out of there as fast as I could."

"Without your shoes."

Selena nodded. "How was I supposed to know he would try to track me down? I mean, what man does that?"

Caly stared at her older sister. The shyest of the five, the one with the least interest in a relationship, Selena had never seen herself as others did—bright, kind, and beautiful. She was the sister who'd do anything for a friend or even a stranger. Few knew she was the one who organized the annual Thanksgiving baskets to those in need, or was the driving force behind the Christmas gift boxes to children who'd have nothing to open without her generosity. Selena went about her life with calm assurance and an abhorrence of anything that would turn the spotlight on her, happy to let others take the credit.

Caly found it easy to understand why Linc Caldwell would be attracted to her.

"So he dropped off the shoes and left?" Caly's voice softened at the distress on Selena's face.

"Not exactly. He invited me to lunch, which went well, then left." She refused to discuss his proposal.

"So why the long face? Maybe he'll become a client. Even if he doesn't, being treated to lunch by an incredibly hot, successful businessman can't hurt."

She has no idea, Selena thought. "No. Can't hurt at all."

******

Driving the shoreline, Linc couldn't believe he'd invited Selena to accompany him to Spokane. Never one to feel he needed a woman on his arm, especially one as guileless as Selena Kerrigan, he'd intended to attend the event solo, not wanting any distractions. When he did date, the women always knew the situation, had as much experience as he, and didn't expect more than a few dinners followed by passionate sex—at their place. Their lack of desire for a relationship mirrored his. His attraction to Selena couldn't be more out of place.

It hadn't been hard to peg her as someone who rarely drank or partied. The way she'd inserted herself into the group's conversation on real estate intrigued and amused him. He'd found himself wanting to protect her. From what, he didn't know. Maybe herself.

Several hours after she passed out in his bed, he'd settled beside her, propping himself on one arm, watching her as she slept. Forcing himself to turn away, it had taken a long time for sleep to claim him, only to wake and find her gone. The sense of loss shook him.

Linc had been through one relationship that rocked his belief in forever after, changing the way he felt about commitment and faithfulness. It had taken time to come to terms with the mistake he'd made. Pouring himself into his work as a SEAL, spending his time off with teammates, and swearing off commitment, he'd carved a comfortable niche that had served him well.

After all he'd been through and the defenses he'd built, how could a few brief moments with a woman leave such a strong impression on him? When he found she'd disappeared, Linc had made up his mind to find her and get her out of his system. After seeing her today, he realized how ill-prepared he was to make that happen.

Parking his truck in front of his office, Linc grabbed the ringing phone, holding it to his ear as he strolled toward the TSR offices, not too concerned at the news from his former SEAL teammate. Tomás "Phreaker" Vega, the best computer expert and hacker Linc had ever met, filled him in on what he'd learned.

"So far, whoever it is hasn't gotten much. I'd say the threat level is low."

"Keep searching. The hacker's intentions could change in a minute."

"Will do."

"Thanks, Phreaker. Stay in touch."

"Hey, man. You know I hate that name," Vega protested, his voice a low growl. "It's so damn old school."

Linc chuckled as his friend clicked off. He missed working with his team. Hell, he missed everything about being a SEAL Platoon Commander, but he'd never been one to sit around licking his wounds.

Stopping outside the office entrance, he scanned the area, the same as he did each time he stepped inside. Hidden in the woods a few miles from the north end of Lake Bountiful, the nondescript TSR building seemed innocuous from the outside. Inside, however, it housed state of the art security and monitoring equipment, some of it not yet available for public use. His contacts within the government allowed TSR to beta test new entries into the security and rescue industry long before competitors knew of its existence. This element alone, testing cutting edge technology, allowed them to hire the best. The company's success had everything to do with the people within this building, and he never let them forget it. Their accomplishments depended on each member of his civilian crew, much as it had in his SEAL team.

"Hey, Linc. I didn't know you'd gotten back." Matt walked up, handing him a printout of recent contracts. "Take a look." Matt's broad smile already told Linc all he needed to know.

"Four wins out of five submittals." He glanced up. "I expected nothing less."

"That's all you have to say?" Matt's incredulous voice followed Linc as he turned toward his office. "This is incredible. Who wins eighty percent of their proposals in this industry? And may I remind you, we've been between seventy-five and eighty percent for six months now."

Looking over his shoulder, Linc shot him a measured look. "Then I guess we should go for a hundred percent."

Matt crossed his arms, staring, as Linc disappeared into his office, closing the door.

"Don't let it bother you, man." Shane joined Matt in the hallway. "Linc doesn't understand why we don't win every submittal. That's just his nature and why we're so successful. Never give up and never settle for second place. Winning is everything to him. Has been since high school."

During their junior and senior years in high school, the three had been inseparable. After graduation, Linc left for the Naval Academy, Matt accepted a football scholarship to Penn State, joining the school's Army ROTC program, and Shane, after mulling over several offers, decided on Stanford.

They looked up as Linc's door opened and he stuck his head out. "You guys ready to debrief me about why we didn't win the fifth submittal?" He didn't wait for a response before taking a chair at his small conference table.

Mumbling a curse, Matt stalked into the office, Shane not hiding his amusement at his friend's frustration about not being allowed to celebrate a significant accomplishment.

"You know what you need?" Shane asked Matt as they entered Linc's office.

"No, but I'm sure you'll tell me," he grumbled as he took a seat across from Linc.

"A steady girlfriend. A normal woman you can count on to be waiting for you each night. Someone who'll celebrate your wins, commiserate when things fall apart. And either way, screw your brains out."

"You're crazy," Matt snorted. "That kind of woman doesn't interest me. Besides, a woman like that doesn't exist. At least I've never been able to find one."

"You've just been looking in the wrong places. Believe me, they exist, even for a hardcore womanizer like you."

"Go to hell." Matt flashed Shane a disapproving grin, unable to stifle a chuckle.

Linc leaned back in his chair, arms crossed, listening to his friends. Discussing the opposite sex had always been a way for the three of them to cut through tension and cajole each other out of dark moods. Each had experienced his own failures with relationships, swearing off anything more than casual sex—until Shane had become smitten with his current girlfriend.

Unbidden, an image of Selena flashed across his mind, a warm feeling following close behind. Groaning, Linc shook his head, mumbling a curse.

"What's that, man?" Shane asked.

"Nothing." Linc leaned forward, sliding the report in front of him. His gaze moved between the two men. "Let's get started."

Chapter Six

Spokane, Washington

"You look spectacular." Linc let his gaze wander over Selena, taking his time, appreciating the view. They'd had a short flight from Peregrine Bay to Spokane, her saying little, responding in short replies to his attempts at casual conversation. He'd finally backed off, letting her enjoy the brief trip in peace.

Selena smiled at the compliment, the butterflies in her stomach continuing to taunt her. "Thank you. Do you think it's too much?" She slid her hands down the deep red silk dress, not yet comfortable in an outfit so obviously meant to draw attention to every curve. "My sister, Caly, helped me pick it out."

"You'll have to thank her for me. You're nothing short of stunning." Linc held himself in check, doing his best to keep his body from announcing the extent of his approval. He offered his arm. "Shall we?"

Sliding her arm through his, Selena squared her shoulders, wanting to appear as tall as possible when walking beside Linc. At over six feet tall with broad shoulders, he cast an imposing and elegant figure in his striking charcoal gray suit accented with a red silk tie. His dark auburn hair fanned the collar of his suit, and the coarse stubble on his face projected a rakish appearance. Handsome, confident, and polished described Lincoln

Caldwell. Selena had no doubt he'd attract considerable female attention tonight.

When they reached the open elevator door, Linc stepped aside, allowing Selena to proceed him. She took a place against the wall, taking a deep breath, willing herself to be calm. As Caly would say, go with it.

"You seem nervous."

Her gaze shot to Linc's. Seeing his roguish smile, she laughed, feeling the tension begin to slip away.

"I told you. I'm not the social butterfly in the family. Events such as this aren't my usual choice for a Friday night." She felt his hand settle on the small of her back as they reached the lobby. The warmth seeped through the thin layer of silk, causing her to shiver.

"Are you cold?" Linc glanced at her, removing his hand from her back, taking the wrap from her and settling it across her shoulders.

"Thank you." Selena refused to tell him she'd experienced jolts of heat ever since she'd boarded the plane in Peregrine Bay. Not once did she attribute it to the temperature. She might not be as experienced as Linc, but she understood when her body responded to a man. It had been all she could do to keep her composure when he chose to sit next to her on the flight, brushing his leg or shoulder against her numerous times. Movements, she felt certain, which had been deliberate. She just wished she could call them unwelcome.

"Lincoln Caldwell and Ms. Selena Kerrigan," Linc told the lady behind the registration table, taking the name tags and program she offered.

"You're at table three near the front, Mr. Caldwell. You still have time to mingle before dinner is served. Enjoy your evening." The woman shot him a quick, practiced smile before focusing on the next couple in line.

"Tell me again why you chose to attend this event," Selena asked as they entered the large ballroom. A bar anchored each end of the room, tables filling the space in between. She guessed there must be close to three hundred people milling about, or "schmoozing", as her sister Julia would say. Although more comfortable at public appearances than Selena, Julia had her own reasons for wanting to limit the number of civic and social events she attended. She and Adam had been married a few short weeks, changing the priorities in both their lives.

"Right now, my company wins the majority of security contracts in Idaho, as well as Western Washington and Northern Oregon. The best way to keep the business flowing is through personal connections with those who make the decisions." He stopped, turning toward her. "Although I'm certain you understand this as one of the owners of your real estate company."

Her eyes flashed. "How did you know I'm an owner? My family doesn't give out that kind of information." She crossed her arms, tilting her head to one side.

"I have a very talented person who obtains all kinds of information for me. He discovered a recent document showing your father, Joshua Kerrigan, as the chairman of Kerrigan Real Estate & Property Management, Julia Kerrigan Monroe as the President, Calypso Kerrigan as the Vice President of property management, and Selena Kerrigan as the Vice President of real estate sales. All four of you own various percentages of the company. That leaves your youngest sisters, Danielle and Lillian. What are their roles at the company?"

Selena stared at him, wide-eyed. Although most people in town knew the three oldest Kerrigan sisters ran the everyday operations of the business, few knew their father had made arrangements for each to own a percentage, allowing them to share in the profits. She suspected the action assured their father each would give their maximum effort to grow the company. Luckily for him, his oldest daughters enjoyed and flourished in the real estate business.

"That information is confidential. Besides our family, only our lawyer and accountant know of Father's arrangement with us. How did you…" Her voice trailed off as she noted the gleam in his eye. "You *didn't* know, did you? You were taking a wild guess and pulled me in," she huffed out, taking a step forward, placing her palm on his chest. "You should be ashamed of yourself."

Holding up his hands in surrender, Linc flashed her a smile, melting her irritation and sending alarms through her body. "Guilty as charged. As you said, I took a wild guess to see what you'd say. It was a calculated risk with a fifty percent chance of going in my favor."

"I can see I'll need to be extremely careful around you." Selena let her hand drop to her side, but not before noticing the solid wall of muscle under the chic gray suit. Her mind conjured up a sexy image of him without his coat and shirt. She wondered if the reality matched her imagination.

Taking her hand in his, Linc brought it to his lips, brushing a soft kiss across her knuckles. "I hope you won't be too careful," he teased, releasing her hand, again resting his on the small of her back. He guided her toward the nearest bar, making casual conversation and introductions as he took a place in line. "What would you like to drink?"

"Ginger ale, or tea, or—"

"Not a martini?" His eyes sparkled.

"Certainly not. I assure you, there will be no repeat performance of that night."

He ordered their drinks, then turned back to her. "That may be the saddest declaration I've heard in a long time. You didn't find my party enjoyable or entertaining?" His expression changed to a mock pout.

Despite her best efforts, Selena laughed. "The party was wonderful, the music and people entertaining, at least as far as I remember through the stupor I created for myself."

"And what of my bed. Did you also find it unappealing?" He tilted his glass toward her, then took a sip of his scotch, his gaze never leaving hers.

"Well, no...I mean, yes." She touched a hand to her cheek, feeling the skin heat. "What I mean is, I'm sure it's quite comfortable. Unfortunately, I wasn't in any shape to enjoy it." She groaned the moment the words left her lips, hoping he didn't catch her slip.

"Well, that's something we can easily rectify."

Her breath caught as her teeth clenched together.

"You name the night, and I'll do my best to ensure you have a night full of enjoyment in my bed."

"Alone?" she squeaked out.

His laughter emerged, rich and deep. "Of course not. I'll need to give you my personal, undivided attention. I wouldn't want you to suffer sleeping in such a big bed alone, perhaps becoming disoriented and stumbling out of the house without all your possessions."

Her jaw worked, but nothing came out. If Caly were here, she'd have a perfect retort, put Linc in his place, and move on to another topic. All Selena could do was lock onto his hypnotic blue eyes, now sparking with amusement. Her mind went completely blank, except for the images emerging of them naked, him hovering over her as he took her mouth in a scorching kiss.

Shaking her head, Selena tipped back her glass of soda, downing half the contents while still focusing on his magnetic eyes. They seemed to penetrate beyond normal awareness, finding her weaknesses, discovering layers she'd rather keep hidden. Watching him study her, she could easily understand how he'd be a formidable opponent on a battlefield or in a boardroom. Without a doubt, the man was way beyond her league.

"Selena Kerrigan, right?" The voice behind her triggered a vague recollection. Turning, she gasped, recognizing the man she hoped to never see again.

"Chad Donovan…" Her voice trailed off as she recalled the last time she'd seen him. His back to her, naked, the room crammed with spectators as the cameras rolled. "It's, uh…good to see you again." She glanced at Linc, noting the set of his jaw, his gaze narrowed at Chad. "Linc, Chad and I attended college together. Chad, this is Lincoln Caldwell."

Chad extended his hand. "Nice to meet you." He didn't add he already knew about Linc and his company, a competitor to his stepfather's firm. The surprise was finding Selena with him. Shifting back to her, he didn't hide his obvious interest, his gaze wandering over the tight red dress. He had no idea what had been hidden under all the layers of clothes she wore in college. "I didn't know you lived in Spokane."

"She doesn't." Linc didn't hide his irritation at Chad's obvious interest in Selena. "We flew up from Peregrine Bay for tonight's event."

Chad took a slight step back, glancing between the two. "As I recall, that's where your family lives, correct?" He directed the question at Selena, ignoring the negative vibes from her date. There had been two reasons Ephraim sent him to Spokane to attend the dinner. One, to become more acquainted with the leaders in the city's building industry, and two, to meet Linc Caldwell. A quick review of TSR's website had announced them as one of the sponsors of the event. It had been a lucky guess that Linc would be in attendance. Finding Selena with him was a pleasant surprise.

"You have a good memory. What are you doing these days?" Selena had heard the stories about Chad moving to California to continue what he'd started in college. It hadn't surprised her. She now realized her reaction to what she'd witnessed the night of their graduation had been due to her sheltered life and naiveté, as well as being completely unprepared for what she saw. Embarrassment still washed over her when she thought of how she'd fled to the bathroom, losing the small amount of food in her stomach. Still, it wasn't something she wanted to witness again.

"I recently moved back home from California to take a job with my stepfather's company. My territory includes Washington and Idaho." He didn't elaborate. "Feels good to return."

The dinner announcement had Linc stepping forward, cupping Selena's elbow. "We should find our seats."

"It was good to see you, Selena. I'll make it a point to call when I'm in Peregrine Bay in a few weeks." Chad leaned forward, placing a kiss on her cheek, not noticing her flinch at his touch. "Linc, it was a pleasure."

"Perhaps we'll see each other again." Linc turned to lead Selena away.

"Oh, you can count on it." Chad shoved his hands in his pockets, watching as they took seats at one of the front tables. He'd already planned a trip to Peregrine Bay to meet with an old friend. Now he had more than one reason for making the journey.

******

Selena felt the tension crackle between her and Linc during dinner, wondering what had caused his change in mood. Her gracious, teasing escort had become quiet and watchful. Several times, she noticed his gaze fixed on Chad a few tables away.

"Did you date him in college?"

Selena swung her gaze toward Linc, startled at the question. "Not that it's your business, but no, we never dated. We sat near each other in a couple classes, shared notes a few times, but he rarely acknowledged me outside of class."

"But you wanted him to." Linc's interest in her relationship with Chad surprised him. Rarely did a woman pique his curiosity as much as Selena.

"At one time, yes. But I learned some things about him that changed my mind. Besides, Chad had what you could call his own fan club. Both men and women were drawn to his open, outgoing personality. He always seemed to be up for anything." She winced at the unintentional double meaning in her words.

"I take it you weren't one of his groupies." Linc took the last bite of his mystery chicken, setting down his fork.

"Hardly. The only time I ever saw him socially was after my graduation dinner with my family. He invited me to a party at a private home." She took a sip of wine, a wry smile twisting her mouth.

"Your one and only date with Chad?" Linc leaned toward her. The thought of her going out with Chad left a ball of ice in his stomach.

"Again, no. When I arrived, he introduced me to a few people, then left to find his own pleasures. I didn't speak to him again that night and haven't seen him until this evening, although I had heard he'd moved to California." He'd somehow obtained her cell number and left a couple messages, which she never returned.

Intrigued, Linc leaned closer. "Any idea what he does?"

"Well…" She fiddled with the napkin in her lap, trying to decide how much to tell him.

"Don't tell me. Let me guess. He robs banks."

She glanced up. "No."

"Became a mime at Venice Beach?"

Laughing, she shook her head.

"A host at a theme park?" Linc's brow arched.

Shaking her head, she moved closer, her lips an inch from his ear. "He became a porn star."

His deep bark of laughter drew attention from several tables around them. Selena could feel her cheeks heat, sensing several pairs of eyes on them.

"Shush."

"Why?" He reached over, taking her hand in his. "You have nothing to be embarrassed about. He chose the profession, not you. From what I know, it can be quite lucrative."

Her gaze snapped to his. "You know others who make those movies?"

"In fact, I do. I went to high school with one, and served in the Navy with another. As far as I know, they're both still making porn flicks, socking away tons of money, and have no regrets." He signaled their server for more coffee. "Actually, the flicks aren't bad."

"You've seen them?" Her brows arched at his comment.

His eyes glistened at the surprise in her voice. "We provided protection for one of them when a fan decided to become a stalker. When he sent our fee, we found a couple movies tucked in the package." He grinned, taking a sip of coffee. "Hey, I'm only human. What's a guy to do?"

"Return them?"

"No way. My partners, Matt and Shane, broke out the beer and we made a night of it."

Her voice lowered to a whisper. "Were they any good?"

"Total crap, but we had a good time. I think Shane donated them to the local library."

Her eyes widened in shock. "He did not."

He shook his head, lifting her hand to his lips and placing a soft kiss on her knuckles. "No, he didn't." Linc flashed her one of his killer smiles as the emcee stepped up to the microphone to begin the program. "If you're curious, I can find out—"

"No," she hissed, glancing around at their tablemates. "Forget I ever asked."

Threading her fingers through his, he tilted his head. "Of course," he answered, knowing he wouldn't.

******

Selena worked to keep her attention on the presentations and speakers instead of Linc sitting next to her, his thigh making contact with hers, his hand resting on her knee under the table. So far, the evening had been nothing like she expected.

Linc wanted her to accompany him, but not as a date, which would've distracted him from the business reasons for his attending. Somehow, his request had taken a dive the moment she'd opened her door to see him standing in the hall, his blatant perusal of her causing fissures in her carefully concealed desire. Never had she felt such strong strokes of heat for a man, stripping away the shy façade she hid behind.

"It shouldn't be much longer." Linc's fingers squeezed her leg lightly, causing her to glance up to see him lean closer, his breath fanning her cheek. "We'll stay a little while, then disappear."

Selena could feel her face heat at his implied meaning, forcing herself not to read too much into it. Despite her best efforts, she did. It had been far too long since she'd allowed herself to feel anything for a man. Her entire focus since college had been on work, proving to her father and oldest sister, Julia, she deserved a chance. According to both, as well as her position in the company, she'd succeeded. The few dates she'd allowed herself over the years hadn't progressed beyond friendship. There'd never been the passion she'd witnessed between Julia and Adam, making her doubt herself capable of such deep emotions.

If her body's response to Linc was any indication, she'd been wrong.

"Don't feel we must leave because of me. After all, you're one of the sponsors." It was an obligatory response, allowing him a reason to stay.

"Believe me, Selena, this is *not* where I want to be tonight." His deep blue eyes darkened as his gaze held hers.

A round of applause pulled their attention to the podium as the speaker stepped down and the band began to play. Linc stood, holding out his hand. "Dance with me, Selena."

She bit her lower lip, thinking how long it had been since she'd danced. All the Kerrigan sisters had taken ballroom dance classes. Of the five, Caly had shown the most aptitude while Selena floundered, never seeming to hear the beat. Fear swept over her.

"I'm not very good and I certainly don't want to embarrass you. Perhaps someone else..." Her gaze darted around the room.

"Trust me. You'll do fine." Linc's confidence wrapped around her as she placed her hand in his.

"Don't say I didn't warn you."

His soft chuckle preceded his quiet voice at her ear. "There's nothing you could do to embarrass me." Turning Selena, he took her in his arms. "All you have to do is follow me. And relax." His mouth tipped up into a warm smile.

******

One dance became two, then five. After almost twenty minutes, Selena had to beg off. Taking her elbow, Linc guided her back to their table.

"Ladies and gentlemen, it's been a pleasure sharing a table with you this evening." Linc handed Selena her purse. "Enjoy the music."

She had a scant second to say her goodbyes before Linc swept her from the room, heading to the elevators and ushering her inside. No one joined them, the mirrored walls closing around them. The doors had barely shut when Linc turned her to him, cupped her face with both hands, and lowered his head.

"I've been wanting to do this all night." His gaze searched her face, giving Selena a moment to pull away before he pressed his lips to hers.

Nothing had ever felt as wonderful as his lips on hers, taking control, demanding she respond. With no hesitation, she wrapped her arms around his neck, her fingers slipping through his silky hair, drawing him down.

His lips traced a path from the corner of her mouth, along the line of her jaw, to the sensitive spot below her ear, his breath igniting a shudder of desire throughout her body. Heat flooded her as his hands splayed across her back, aligning their bodies, shifting to pull her closer.

When the elevator signaled their floor, Linc broke the kiss. He dropped his hands from her back and grabbed her hand, entwining their fingers. Leading Selena to his room, he opened the door and drew her inside. Turning her to him, he settled his hands on her shoulders.

"I want you, Selena, but I won't rush you. If this is too soon for you…"

His ragged voice trailed off as her hands settled on his chest, then wrapped around his waist. Leaning up, she brushed a soft, tentative kiss across his mouth, then gazed up into eyes that had gone from brilliant blue to deep cobalt.

Selena's overactive mind told her it was too soon. She didn't know him and certainly didn't love him. Her body, however, sent a different message, telling her to jump in, explore the passion she felt for this man. Taking risks, pushing herself beyond her self-imposed boundaries had never been easy. But she wanted to explore what could happen with Linc. Take a chance.

"I want to stay." She swallowed, her gaze dropping to his chest.

Placing a finger under her chin, he drew her face back up to his. "What is it, Selena?"

Her cheeks colored slightly, her tongue darting out to moisten lips still sensitive from his kisses. "It's been a long time. I don't know…" She shook her head, unable to continue as his finger traced a line from her chin up her cheek, then cupped it.

"We'll take it as slow as you want." He leaned down, brushing his lips across hers.

She closed her eyes, feeling a surge of fear at embarrassing herself in front of the only man she'd felt anything for in years. Her few experiences hadn't left her with anything close to personal satisfaction, doing nothing for her confidence.

"I just don't want you to be disappointed."

"Ah, sweetheart. Trust me. You could never disappoint me." He kicked the door closed when he saw her slight nod, then swept her into his arms. "Our first time will not be against a wall, on the floor, or on a cramped sofa." He walked through an interior door of his suite, then set her down next to a canopied bed covered with a thick, ivory-colored spread and tapestry pillows in browns, beiges, and deep reds. He chuckled, seeing her eyes widen as she looked around the large room. "I know. It's a little over the top."

She shook her head, then turned back to him, smiling. "It's gorgeous. I had no idea they offered rooms like this one."

"I have to admit that when I made the reservation, I hoped you'd join me here."

"A little presumptuous, don't you think?"

Linc ran his hands up her arms, letting his fingers linger on her soft skin. "Did I hope for too much?" His voice, husky and deep, sent shivers through her body.

Heat flooded her as she let him draw her closer. "No, Linc, you didn't."

He smiled, letting out a breath as he pulled her close, claiming her mouth. Softly, his lips played against hers, encouraging her to open before he plunged inside, teasing and tasting. His arms tightened around her, kissing her as if he never wanted to let her go.

Selena moaned as the heat of his body burned through the thin silk of her dress, creating a tightness deep in her belly. Blood thrummed through her, sending waves of fire from her toes to her face. She could feel her body tremble as his hand moved to her hip, then lower, drawing up the hem of her short dress, stroking her thigh.

He drew back, his breathing deep and ragged, his gaze locking with hers. "Last chance to change your mind," he whispered.

Need speared through her at the look of raw desire on his face. She smiled, wrapping her hands behind his neck, drawing him down. "I want you, Linc."

It was all the answer he needed. With a deep, pleasure-filled groan, he scooped her into his arms, settling her on the bed, then stretched out beside her. "I hope you're prepared for a long, sleepless night." He slid a hand through her hair, capturing her sigh with a scorching kiss.

Chapter Seven

Sipping her flavored ice tea, Selena laughed at the text message Linc sent. Looking back at the last month, she acknowledged her fear of a relationship with him may have been misplaced. He'd been nothing short of amazing since their first night in Spokane. She felt her face heat as she remembered their night of lovemaking, which continued once they'd returned to Peregrine Bay. Even with their busy schedules and having to drive between the north and south shores, they still saw each other several nights each week. She didn't know where their relationship was headed, but she'd made up her mind to enjoy the journey.

"Selena? Are you with us?" Julia sent Selena an amused glance as Caly tapped her fingernails on the desk, arching a brow. "If we can get your undivided attention, we *might* be able to finish up before the office closes."

"Sorry." She slid her phone back into her pocket. "Where were we?"

Julia shook her head, her mouth tipping up into a smile. "Caly reviewed the new property management clients we've picked up in the last thirty days. Did you have any comments?"

"None."

"All right. Now it's your turn to go over the recent listings and sales, then I'll talk about our new business development program." Julia settled back in her chair, enjoying Selena's slight discomfort. In reality, she couldn't be happier for her sister, although she had serious concerns about Selena jumping so quickly into what appeared to be a relationship. Her behavior was out of character. For a woman who rarely dated, preferring the company of a book to socializing, she'd fallen hard for a man with a reputation as a serious player. If Linc did anything to hurt Selena, he'd face some serious and undisguised anger from the other Kerrigan sisters.

"That's it. An uptick in listings and three more sales than projected for last month. I do have a recommendation, however." Selena shot a look at Caly.

Julia nodded for her to continue.

"We have three salespeople and are in desperate need of at least one more. Caly, you've mentioned a few times about getting into sales. You have your license. Would you like to take on walk-in buyers to get your feet wet?"

Caly shuffled the papers in her hand, pretending to consider the option, knowing she'd love to combine sales with her property management responsibilities. "It depends. How many walk-ins do we get in a week?"

"In the summer, there could be as many as a dozen, with perhaps three converting to actual buyers. Between Halloween and Easter, it tapers off to maybe one or two a week." Selena shifted in her seat, feeling her phone vibrate in her pocket, wondering if Linc had sent another text. "What do you think?"

"I'd like to give it a try with one condition. I'd take no more than two actual buyers per month. With everything else I have going, I think that's all I can handle." Caly could feel her excitement growing. She'd begun to stagnate doing just property management, craving the stimulation making sales provided while introducing new residents to her wonderful community.

"Done," Julia said, casting a hard look at Caly. "But you'll need to be in the same rotation system we use for all the salespeople. You won't be able to pick and choose, or hand someone off to another agent."

"No problem. I'll take whomever comes my way."

"That's it then. I'll see you both at dinner tonight," Julia commented.

"Sorry, Julia. I'm afraid I have a date and won't be able to make it. Next time?" Caly stood, pushing her chair toward the table.

"No worries. And Selena, please bring Linc. Adam plans to be there and he'd love some male company."

"I'll do my best."

Selena hurried down the hall, pulling her phone out of her pocket. As expected, a text from Linc awaited her. She smiled at his question.

Where do you want to meet for dinner?

******

"What is it?" Shane moved up behind Matt, scanning the computer screen that held his friend's attention.

"I'm not certain." He pursed his lips, trying to decipher the information sent to him by Tomás Vega. "Phreaker must be working overtime. He's sent three warnings in the last hour about some threat to our security." Matt picked up the phone, dialing Linc's number. "Pick up, boss," he muttered as the phone continued to ring. More than an hour earlier, Linc had dashed out of the office, heading for a meeting in Peregrine Bay, telling them not to expect him back. Matt left a brief message when his call went to voicemail.

"A client or here at the office?" Shane asked, pulling up a chair.

"Bennington Technology."

Shane mumbled an oath. "That's the second client in the last two weeks, and they're our two largest."

"And both are in the software application industry." Matt sent a reply to Vega's latest message.

"So far, neither has sustained a full breach, but these two attempts came close. Phreaker usually identifies a couple each month and shuts them down. As you can see, the attacks are getting stronger and more frequent." Shane pointed to a trending chart showing the number of breach attempts over the last few months.

"Could be a determined competitor. Maybe one of the companies we're up against for the arts center project wants to make it appear we've done a lousy job."

Matt leaned forward, concentrating on the latest message from Phreaker. "He's shut this one down and is trying to get the source. They all seem to lead to a dead end."

Shane scrubbed a hand down his face. "If anyone can sort it out, it's Phreaker. I'll set up a conference call for tomorrow morning about eight o'clock between you, Linc, Phreaker, and me."

"You'd better make it nine. Linc hasn't been getting into the office as early as usual," Matt snickered. "I think our boy is a goner."

"No doubt. I've never known him to be so obsessed with a woman. Unless you include—"

"Don't even go there, Shane. She was a mistake he'd rather forget."

"At least it was short-lived with no lasting consequences. It could've been worse." Matt finished a message to Phreaker, then stood, following Shane into the hall. "Much worse."

******

"You mean you've been able to dig up nothing on Linc Caldwell or his partners?" Greg Nelson didn't try to hide his disgust. Simondson Security's head of cyber investigations met his boss's gaze. They'd had a month to come up with anything they could use to discredit TSR. So far, all their work had been for nothing.

"Hard to imagine, but those boys are squeaky clean. Linc's service record is damn near perfect, and his partners have nothing more than a couple speeding tickets. We'll keep looking."

"Any luck breaking into their system?" Greg crossed his arms, leaning back in his chair. He'd known finding anything on the TSR partners would be difficult, but felt it was worth the chance.

"None. Whoever is in charge of their cyber security is top-notch."

Greg stared at the man, considering what he'd said. "Find out who he or she is. Seems we might want to make an offer that would be hard to refuse."

"Sure thing, boss. Anything else?"

"No. We'll just have to find other ways to beat our competition." Although Greg didn't quite know how.

They'd sharpened their pencils as much as possible on the arts center bid. He knew his boss, Ephraim Simondson, had his own ideas on how to win the bid. His methods included putting pressure on Tom Harten, a Peregrine Bay councilman, to do what he could to obtain the award for Simondson. Greg suspected Ephraim's stepson, Chad, had been hired to do just that. Greg was all for using a competitor's weaknesses against them, but he drew the line at doing anything that hinted at coercion or bribery. Unfortunately, Ephraim didn't share his view.

******

"The latest attempts are coming through a server in Indonesia. Probably a public café or other open network location. It doesn't mean the person or persons trying to access their computer system is actually in Indonesia. That information could take weeks or months to pin down."

Linc held the phone closer to his ear, his mind immediately going to Simondson Security in Portland. He walked out of the kitchen where Julia and Selena finished preparing dinner while waiting for Adam. "Can you identify anything else?" he asked Phreaker.

"Nope. I've already connected with Matt. We have a conference call set up for nine tomorrow, but there's not much more I can tell you. At this point, I haven't been able to identify who's trying to hack in, but you know me. I won't rest until I find out as much as possible."

"Thanks. We'll talk tomorrow." Linc hung up, turning at the sound of footsteps behind him.

"Everything all right?" Selena walked up, resting a hand on his arm.

"Nothing important." He pulled her into his arms, burying his face in her hair. "I missed you today." He moved his lips to her neck, nuzzling the sensitive spot below her ear. "Is it too late to beg off and go to your place?"

She pulled back, laughing. "Yes, it is. Besides, I know how much you like to eat, and I certainly wouldn't want lack of food to affect your stamina." She cocked a brow.

Linc grabbed her around the waist, hauling her back to him. "As if." He lowered his mouth, brushing a soft kiss across her lips, then deepening it.

They broke away when Julia cleared her throat behind them. "I hate to interrupt, but Adam just got home." She sent them a knowing smile before returning to the kitchen.

"All right. You win." Linc took her hand in his, following the voices to see Adam and Julia in a similar pose, arms wrapped around each other.

"So, what about dinner?" Selena asked.

Letting Julia go, Adam grinned at Selena before looking at Linc. "Glad you two could make it. Sorry I'm late. We had another prowler at the site of the new arts center. I hope they start framing the building soon."

Linc caught Julia's eye, knowing they were both thinking the same thing. "I know this isn't the place, but when do you think the committee will make a decision on the security contract?" he asked.

"No, it's not the place, but I understand your frustration at not having a decision." Julia sighed, wishing she could award the contract to the lowest bidder, which happened to be Linc's company. They also had the references and experience for jobs several times the size of the work in Peregrine Bay. "We meet again at the end of the week. The mayor and I have already made our recommendation. Tom Harten is the one holding it up. The man is a constant pain when it comes to city awards." She picked up her glass of wine and took a slow sip. "There's a new person in town representing Simondson Security. Tom wants to meet with him before making his final decision. Besides Tom, the unknowns are the two citizen members of the committee, although the mayor told me he discussed the proposals with them and is pleased with the firm they want to support." She nodded at Linc, hoping he got the message.

"Enough discussing work. Let's eat." Adam placed an arm around Julia's shoulders, turning her toward the kitchen.

Selena slid her arm through Linc's, raising her brow. "What do you think she meant by that?"

"If I had to guess, I'd say your sister just told me TSR has four votes. If that's the case, it won't matter who Harten supports." *Unless our current clients are experiencing security breaches, which could be a game changer*, Linc thought. Knowing his employees were working around the clock to thwart the latest threats, he shook his head. No use borrowing trouble.

"Do you know the Simondson representative Julia mentioned?" Linc asked.

Selena shook her head. "I have no idea."

They'd talked a great deal about their jobs. Selena wanted to know everything she could about him. His candor when sharing his past surprised her. Most men seemed to offer little, especially when their experiences included working in war zones.

She'd been fascinated when he'd confessed he'd never been in love, never had anyone truly special in his life. He'd shrugged it off as not having time between his years at the Naval Academy, tours of duty oversees, then building his company.

She looked up, brushing her mouth against his, the rumbling of his stomach causing Selena to laugh against his lips.

"Sounds like we'd better get you fed."

******

"What seems to be the problem at the site of the arts center?" Linc sipped his coffee, glancing at Adam as the women chatted on the other side of the room.

"Nothing major. Since the excavation started, a few of our homeless have taken up residence in the deep holes to ward off the chill. They're usually gone as soon as the sun comes up. Tonight, one took over a piece of equipment, setting up his sleeping bag and hanging his belongings all over the cab." Adam chuckled, remembering the site as he and one of his officers drove up. "I never saw anything quite like it."

"Did you arrest him?" Linc watched as Selena and Julia walked down the hall, disappearing into one of the bedrooms. He'd hoped to get her home, join her in bed, and pleasure her until they fell asleep from exhaustion. Instead, he'd be driving back to his office, hoping to discover the source and reason for the attempts to break into his clients' computers.

"If you can believe it, the guy offered me a drink from his bottle. Almost fell out of the cab when he bent over to hand it to me." Adam smiled as he recalled the man trying to keep his balance. "I decided it was in his best interest to sleep it off in a warm, secure cell. I also called the general contractor. He's going to set up around the clock security."

"That will take care of most intruders. Once the foundation is poured, the work should progress quickly." Linc kept his gaze on the back room where Selena had disappeared. His body tightened when he heard her warm, clear laugh through the open door.

The intensity of his feelings for her bothered Linc more than he cared to admit. He never expected the woman who'd passed out in his bed would be the one to capture his heart, disarming him with her sincerity, warmth, and honesty. One relationship misstep had convinced him his passion would be better served investing it in his work. The result had been a successful company, as well as a series of short-term arrangements with women he enjoyed, even liked, but never connected with on a deeper level. The effortless way Selena had broken through all his defenses in a few short weeks stunned him.

Adam leaned forward in his chair, cradling his coffee between his hands, noting the way Linc kept shifting his gaze to the hallway. "How are things going?"

Linc turned his attention back to Adam, wondering if he meant his business or relationship with Selena. "Better than anticipated. We've landed a couple new contracts. I'm hoping we'll get the okay on the art center after the meeting Julia mentioned. I have nothing to complain about."

"Heard from Dez?" Adam asked, glancing over the rim of his cup. He referred to Linc's older brother, a graduate of West Point and member of Special Forces. At least he was when Adam met him during one of Dez's infrequent visits with Linc a few years before.

"It's been over two years. I have a bead on where he is, but…" Linc clamped his mouth shut, the tensing of his jaw signaling his frustration.

"They'd have notified your parents if anything had happened. He's probably being sent on one mission after another with no time to get in touch."

"Right. Try telling that to my mom and dad," Linc groused, anger lacing his words.

Adam let it pass, deciding to change subjects. "How's it going with Selena?"

Linc locked eyes on his friend. "Good."

Adam didn't respond as his gaze narrowed on Linc. "More coffee?" He stood, walking to the kitchen, Linc coming up behind him. He filled both their cups, then leaned a hip against the counter.

"She told Julia you've never been married. Did you tell Selena that?" His voice hardened, the question accusatory.

Taking a deep breath, Linc leaned against the opposite counter. "That's what I led her to believe," he sighed, remembering the night Adam and he had downed more beers than he could recall.

Adam had still been a detective in Spokane, working on a homicide in the home of one of Linc's clients. They'd each let their guard down, Adam recalling his regret about walking away from the only woman he'd ever loved, and Linc admitting to a brief instant of insanity when he'd married after a whirlwind affair. Neither had spoken of their admissions since.

"Why? If you told her the circumstances and result, you know she would understand."

"She asked if I'd ever been in love. I told her no, which is true. If she'd asked if I'd ever been in *lust*, I would've said yes. Frankly, it's been years. I haven't heard from the woman since she got a quickie divorce while I was deployed." Linc finished the coffee, setting the cup on the counter. "Trust me. I didn't spend time grieving the breakup."

"I believe you, but will Selena? I know these Kerrigan women pretty well, and lies of omission don't set well with them. Unless this is a short-term fling for you. If that's the case, you and I will need to have some serious words." Adam crossed his arms, his gaze hardening.

Linc glared at his friend, but didn't respond as the sound of Selena's laughter preceded her into the kitchen.

She came to an abrupt stop when she saw the severe expressions on the men's faces.

"Everything all right?" Selena walked up to Linc, touching his arm.

Linc broke eye contact with Adam, his face softening as he looked down at Selena. "Everything's fine. Are you ready to leave?"

Feeling the tension between Linc and Adam, she picked up her coat and purse. "Ready." She gave Julia a hug, then took the hand Linc offered.

"Thank you for including me tonight. Dinner was great." Linc glanced at Adam, knowing the subject wasn't over. He knew he needed to discuss the past with Selena, but it wouldn't happen tonight. Not with the threats to TSR clients.

"I hope you'll consider coming with Selena to our family dinner on Sunday. I know Father and Joannie would love to meet you." Julia winked at Selena. They both knew their father would grill Linc to make sure he was good enough for his daughter, while their stepmother, Joannie, would welcome him with open arms.

"Thanks, Julia. I'll think about it." He glanced at Selena, noting how her expression hadn't changed.

She'd never invited him to the weekly family dinners, and frankly, he didn't know how he felt about going. He liked and cared about her, but didn't know if his feelings were strong enough to signal to her family that they may have a future. The thought had him looking at Adam, whose cool expression conveyed his own thoughts better than any spoken words. Linc had a good deal of thinking and explaining to do. Selena's reaction would determine if they had a future beyond their growing friendship and passionate nights.

✳✳✳✳✳✳

Linc walked her to the front door, having every intention of cutting their night short and returning to his office. When she opened the door, grabbed his hand, and pulled him inside, wrapping her arms around him, his plan disintegrated.

Drawing him toward her, Selena moved her lips against his. His arms tightened around her as he deepened the kiss, taking control.

"I can't stay," he breathed out, his voice growing husky.

"No?" she whispered against his mouth, already moving her hands to the buttons of his shirt. He didn't stop her as she pushed the fabric out of the way, placing her hands on his chest.

Groaning, he tugged her closer before sweeping her into his arms. "Maybe I can stay for a little bit."

Snuggling her face into his neck, she breathed in the scent so unique to Linc. "I think that's a wise decision."

His deep chuckle preceded him placing her in the center of the bed.

"You have too many clothes on." She sat up on her knees, reaching for his belt.

He didn't move as she lowered the zipper and pushed his pants to the ground. As soon as he kicked them off, he wrapped his hands around her wrists. "My turn."

Moments later, he looked at her naked body, his breath catching as it always did when he took in her beauty. "I don't know what you do to me, Selena, but I hope it never ends." He trailed his fingers down her neck to her shoulders, then opened his hand, his warm palm continuing the journey over the curve of her hips, down thighs that quivered at his touch. Stretching out, he wrapped his arms around her, lowering his mouth to capture hers.

All she could do was feel as their tongues tangled, creating ripples of pleasure to spread through her body. The feel of his rough hands caressing her back, then smoothing down her sides to the swell of her hips had her gasping in anticipation.

"I can't wait any longer."

"Then you won't have to." He moved over her, taking it slow until he'd given them both what they wanted.

Chapter Eight

"Anything new?" Linc stepped into Matt's office. He shrugged off his jacket and took a seat, pushing thoughts of his past, and Selena, out of his mind.

After the passionate time in her bed, he'd been reluctant to leave, yet he couldn't put his duties off any longer. Holding her in his arms afterwards, he'd almost given in to Adam's suggestion of disclosing his past marriage. Instead, he'd let his own excuses rule, deciding it might be best to leave the past where it belonged—in the past.

Her immediate understanding about his need to leave triggered a pang of guilt about his decision to keep a marriage of less than a few months to himself. The annulment came while he participated in an extraction mission in Afghanistan. Only his team, family, and a few close friends knew about Valerie and their brief union. As he had driven the dark, winding road to his office, he thought through the pros and cons of telling Selena, deciding to keep the mistake in his past. Despite Adam's warning, he saw no reason to explain his brief error in judgment to her. Valerie was a mistake. Nothing more.

"No. Phreaker is continuing to monitor and trace." Matt shot a look at Linc. "It may be that stopping the threat is the best we can do. Identifying the source may not be the best use of our resources."

Linc had been considering the same. He knew of no one better than Tomás Vega at stopping imminent cyber threats, but he was still just one man. "We may need to hire someone to work with him."

"He won't like it," Matt smirked.

"He'll get used to it. Have any of the clients contacted us?" Linc stood, pacing to the window to look out at a clear night sky filled with stars.

"We've only had two affected, Bennington Technology and Caro Systems, and neither is aware of the attempts. Shane called them on the pretense of asking about our customer service. Each responded positively and appreciated him contacting them." Matt's solemn expression didn't show the relief he felt at the feedback Shane's call provided. "We dodged a bullet."

"For now." Linc turned from the window. "I want to go ahead with our conference call with Vega tomorrow. I'll broach the subject of adding a person to help him."

"Do you have someone in mind?"

"There's a guy I've met from another SEAL team who discharged out a few months ago. He's a tech whiz, like Phreaker, with some serious hostage rescue experience." He picked up his jacket and headed for the door. "That's what might play for Phreaker. We bring the new man on for our rescue division, but make him available on the tech side for special situations such as the one we have now. I'll have all his specifics by our meeting tomorrow."

"Sounds good."

As Linc left the office, Matt turned his attention back to a computer screen showing real-time monitoring of client accounts. TSR had a spotless record. No one had been able to hack their clients' systems, even though numerous attempts had been made.

Employees scanned the monitoring equipment twenty-four hours a day, seven days a week. Linc stopped outside the operations center, watching through the glass windows as the evening crew kept watch on client activity for both divisions. Half the room monitored clients using TSR for computer and systems security. The other half kept track of their rescue service clients.

He stepped aside as the doors pushed open, a young woman dashing out toward Matt's office. Looking up, she stopped.

"Oh, good evening, Mr. Caldwell." She bounced on the balls of her feet, indicating the urgency she felt.

Linc leaned against the doorframe, cocking a brow. "Tina, I've asked you to call me Linc." He remembered she'd left the Army a few months before and still stood on military formalities. She hired on to work in their client rescue division after dual roles in the Army handling public relations and logistics.

"Yes, sir…I mean, Linc."

"Where are you off to in such a rush?"

She glanced at the document in her hand, holding it out to him. "To see Matt. We have a situation."

He quickly scanned it. "Come with me." Taking long strides down the hall, he opened Shane's door. "Meet me in 77C." He moved to Matt's office and said the same. When Tina turned to leave, he stopped her. "You're coming with me."

Her eyes went wide as she followed him through a door to a long hall ending at a conference room reserved for the top executives. Few in the company had ever been in 77C, a room reserved for crises management and operations deployment. The sight caused her breath to hitch. The walls were covered with large monitors focusing on different regions around the globe, while computers and other sophisticated equipment took up most of the desk space.

"What is it?" Matt asked, nodding at Tina as he moved to Linc's side. Shane walked up beside them a moment later, then took a seat in front of a computer.

"An executive with Caro, plus several members of her team, were abducted after a business meeting in Jakarta. The company contacted the U. S. State Department, got nowhere, and then called us." Disgust laced Linc's voice, his jaw set. Caro was one of the two companies Phreaker had spotted with hacking attempts. He didn't like the connection.

Shane muttered a curse as he pulled up a screen showing a detailed map of Jakarta. "They should've called us first."

"Matt, get Phreaker on this. We need Intel *yesterday*," Linc barked out, never taking his eyes off the monitor. "Shane, contact our associates. See who has a team ready to roll as soon as we get the Intel needed."

"Done," Shane answered.

"Tina, I want you to lead the project management on this. Be our voice with the client and any press who snoop around." When she didn't respond, Linc swiveled to see her shocked expression. "Tina, you with me?"

Her gaze snapped to his. "Yes, sir. I'll call the client right away and get every piece of information they have on the hostages." She started to leave.

"You'll work in here with us, Tina." Linc pointed to a seat near Shane. "He'll help with any questions."

"Yes, sir."

"Phreaker's all over it, Linc." Matt stepped next to him, holding out his phone. "Social media is already blowing up over this."

Linc nodded. "Tina, make sure the client has someone experienced handling the media so their executives can work with us without being sidetracked."

"Yes, sir."

Linc pinched the bridge of his nose, a nagging sensation tugging at him. "Shane, don't you have a contact in Jakarta?"

"I've already reached out to him, Linc. He's with the local police in their gangs division. He'll be able to get us the local insight, and even help with logistics if we have to send in a team."

In the rescue industry niche, TSR held a unique position, working with a group of closely connected, yet independent security firms specializing in difficult extractions and hostage rescue.

"Linc, one of our associates has a team finishing up a joint training session in Perth, Australia. They can be ready to roll within hours." Shane continued to type as he spoke, never looking away from the screen. "Hold up," he called over his shoulder. "I've got my contact from Jakarta on the line. He says the police are already on it, suspecting a local gang of the kidnapping. He recommends we hold off sending anyone in until they have more time to evaluate."

"That concurs with the chatter Phreaker is seeing. Let me put him on speaker." Matt reached to a control panel, punching a button, then turning up the volume.

"Phreaker, tell us what you're finding." Linc moved closer to a series of screens showing media coverage of the kidnappings.

"Social media is burning up on this, Linc. The interesting part is what I'm finding out about the movements of Jakarta law enforcement. What I see concurs with Shane's contact. They're targeting a specific gang."

"You hacked their system?" Matt groaned.

"I'm not answering that." There was a pause before Phreaker came back on the line. "Linc, I gotta remind you that Jakarta police *do not* play nice in the sandbox. Sending our own people in could be a monumental mistake."

Linc scrubbed a hand down his face, feeling the longer than normal stubble scrape his fingers, recalling the same incident as Phreaker. Without prior consent of the Indonesian government, their team had been dropped into a hot zone. Thinking they had the support of the local Jakarta police, the SEAL team had continued their mission. The fallout had been swift and the extraction quick. It had been a miracle they'd gotten out of the area with only minor injuries, as well as their target.

"I hear you, man. We'll hold off any action on our end until we know more." Linc glanced to his side. "Tina, get in touch with the client. Give them an update, let them know we are still gathering information, and we have a team ready if the locals come up empty."

Tina glanced up at him, her expression neutral. "Will do, but they're pushing hard for us to do more than talk to them."

"Set up a private call between their CEO and me within the next ten minutes. I'll wait in my office." Linc glanced around the room, taking one more look at the monitors before stepping into the hall. Pulling his phone from a pocket, he checked his messages, surprised to see one from a man he hadn't heard from in years. Someone he'd rather keep in his past. Ignoring his unease at how the man had gotten his private cell number, Linc slid the phone into his pocket. Getting back to the man would have to wait until the current crisis was resolved.

******

Linc rubbed his eyes, pinching the bridge of his nose. The last twenty hours had been difficult. The Intel TSR provided to the Caro CEO had been clear—the local police weren't prepared to deliver a successful rescue. They needed the resources TSR could provide, but several offers of assistance had been refused. The CEO told Linc to hold off, wanting to give the locals a chance to diffuse the situation. Both decisions turned out to be poor choices.

Linc cursed at the latest information flashing across a large monitor in room 77C. He didn't expect to hear from Caro's CEO for a while, knowing he and the rest of his company would be dealing with the deaths of their friends. Of the six taken, four were killed and two severely injured when the police raided the compound where they were held. Twelve gang members had been killed or injured. The police seemed pleased with the outcome.

Glancing at his watch, he felt the familiar sense of fatigue envelope him. His team had been up for over forty-eight hours.

At six o'clock the following evening, it was time to close down and send them home.

"We did all we could. It's time for you all to head out and get some sleep." Linc pursed his lips, his gaze darting among the others. "Thank you for your hard work on this."

"You know we would've stayed no matter how long it took." Shane drew a weary hand over his face, still reeling from the news of the bungled rescue.

"I'd invite everyone to grab a beer, but I'm too tired to make it any further than my place." Matt checked the backup system before shutting down the monitors. "I'll see you all in the morning."

Linc clasped him on the shoulder as Matt opened the door to the hall, stopping when another employee stood ready to knock.

"I heard you were here, Linc." The young man glanced at the others before handing him a note. "I'm sorry to give you another issue, but there's a man standing out front. He's demanding to speak with you and says he won't leave until he does."

Linc let out a deep sigh when he read the man's name. Douglas Bergman, the same man who'd sent him an urgent message almost a day before. Whatever Douglas had to say couldn't be put off any longer. It had to be important if his ex-father-in-law had traveled across the country to see him.

"Escort him to the visitor room and tell him I'll be right there."

"Can't you put him off until you've gotten some sleep?" Matt asked, then looked at the note Linc held out to him. Muttering a curse, he motioned for Shane to take a look.

"Valerie's father?" Shane's eyes widened as his brows shot up.

"The same. He left me a message about the time we learned of the kidnappings. I can't put him off any longer."

"I'll bring coffee into the visitor room for both of you." Tina didn't wait for an answer as she walked down the hall, drawing the attention of the three men.

"You did good hiring her, Matt. I wasn't sold on her background, but she did well during this latest crisis." Linc let out a deep breath, rolling his shoulders, then stretching his arms above his head. "Guess I'd better see what Valerie's father has to say. It had better be worth it."

******

"He hasn't contacted you since after dinner at my place? Isn't that a little odd?" Julia asked as she and Selena walked to their cars. It had been a long day of meetings, including one with the mayor, who presented her with an anonymous message mentioning some disturbing news about TSR. Julia wouldn't mention it to Selena, but she did want to discuss the allegations with Linc.

Selena pulled a key fob from her pocket, the lights on her car flashing when she pressed the button. "It is," she sighed, setting her computer inside. "There's no reason he has to stay in touch. After all, we've only been seeing each other a few weeks and he hasn't made any kind of commitment."

Julia snorted. "Right. If you believe that, you're deluding yourself. From what I've seen, you're both chin deep in a relationship." Seeing Selena's face still, she touched her arm. "Are you two having problems?"

Selena shook her head, her tired gaze sweeping the parking lot. "No. It's just…I'm not sure. Something feels off."

"Look, Adam is working late tonight. Why don't we have dinner and talk?"

"I don't want to mess up your evening, Julia. It's probably nothing more than my insecurities reaching out to bite me."

"First, you won't be messing up my evening, and second, you've always had good instincts. If something seems off with Linc, maybe it is."

"I appreciate the offer, but I think I'd like to head straight home. I'm not very hungry and I have some paperwork to finish up."

"No problem. Call me if you want to talk." Julia hugged her before walking to her own car.

Driving home, Selena thought again of the last conversation between her and Linc. They'd sat in his car outside her home after dinner with Julia and Adam. She knew something weighed on him, deciding to wait until he opened up. He'd stayed silent, escorting her inside, then allowing himself to be drawn into a round of lovemaking. Afterwards, he'd held her. She could sense the tension rolling off him and felt certain whatever bothered him had something to do with her. Reaching up, she'd stroked a finger down his cheek, asking if anything troubled him. Shaking his head, Linc had given her a brief kiss, then crawled from her bed.

Almost two days later, she still hadn't heard from him, which bothered her more than she cared to admit. For weeks, he'd reached out to her two or three times a day, and they'd shared a bed more nights than not. *Maybe it had become too familiar for him,* she worried, walking into her home and locking the door behind her.

Julia was right. Selena's instincts had often saved her from business mistakes and relationship blunders. This time, the problem was she didn't want to consider maybe his feelings were cooling. Not when hers were escalating at a pace she couldn't control. Her heart told her Linc was the one for her, the soul mate she'd always sought. Alas, her intuition warned her otherwise.

Chapter Nine

Linc washed his hands, splashing cold water on his face. He couldn't imagine why Douglas Bergman had a reason to see him after all these years.

Valerie's father hadn't hidden his disapproval of their marriage. He'd never wanted a military man for his only daughter, preferring a doctor, lawyer, or businessman to someone who served their country. As a successful banker, Bergman ruled his home with as much intensity as he did his business. Deep down, Linc always believed Bergman's wishes worked to break down his daughter's determination, creating doubt, leading to the annulment. No matter. The broken marriage had minimal effect on Linc. Within weeks, he'd returned to his old self, feeling no resentment over her decision.

He stopped outside the visitor room, bracing himself for whatever announcement Doug made. Turning the knob, he pushed the door open, coming to a stop when the man he remembered as tall and robust with a dominating personality raised himself from the chair. Gone were the signs of a man in control of his and other's lives. Instead, Linc's gaze wandered over a man of slim build with dull gray hair and slumped shoulders.

"You don't need to stare at me as if I were a skeleton." Douglas extended his hand, wincing at the grip Linc returned.

"Have a seat and tell me why you're here." Linc grimaced at his abrupt words.

"As cocky as ever, I see. Valerie always did say you had more self-confidence than common sense." A pained expression crossed Douglas's face before he controlled his features and settled back into the chair.

"I take it she didn't accompany you today." Linc took a seat across from him and leaned forward, his arms resting on the table.

Douglas studied him a moment, a muscle in his jaw twitching. "I guess you haven't heard. Valerie is dead."

Linc's eyes widened, his lips parting as he blinked back the surprise. "I'm sorry, Douglas. I had no idea. What happened?"

He brushed Linc off with a wave of his hand. "A car crash. The doctors said she didn't suffer." Douglas cleared his throat. "It's been years. We've honored her wishes for a long time. Believe me, if circumstances didn't demand I be here, I'd be home in my easy chair, a big fire heating the room."

Linc studied him, his brows knitting in confusion. "Her wishes? Circumstances? I'm sorry, but you're going to have to spell this all out for me."

"All right. As I'm certain you suspect, the annulment was my idea, not my daughter's. She was beautiful and compassionate, but too weak for a man like you."

"You mean a man dedicated to his job in the military."

"No, I mean too weak for someone as forceful and competitive as you. I knew it would never work. It took a few weeks until my concerns succeeded in changing her mind and she agreed to end the marriage. I helped her file the papers." Douglas glanced up, his bushy eyebrows doing nothing to hide the intensity in his stare. "Unfortunately, I miscalculated."

"What do you mean?"

"A few weeks later, we learned she was pregnant."

Pregnant. The blood drained from Linc's face, his jaw going slack.

"She made the decision to keep the fact from you. I agreed, believing your job precluded you from being a fit father."

"She had an abortion…" Linc's voice trailed off as pain rippled through him, wrenching his heart. An anger stronger than he'd ever known began to build, wrapping its tentacles around him and squeezing.

"Hell no. She never would've agreed to that. Valerie had a baby boy."

For the first time, Linc noticed the sheen in Douglas's eyes as he swiped at the unwanted dampness. "She had two years with him before she died four years ago."

Linc moved his hands to the arms of his chair, gripping so tight his knuckles grew white.

"Where. Is. He?" Linc tried to rein in his anger as he stood, bracing his hands on the table and leaning toward Douglas.

Glaring back at Linc, Douglas felt a sense of relief at getting the response he'd wanted. "You'll see him once I finish. Now, sit down."

Instead, Linc straightened, pacing a few feet away, then turned toward Bergman, his arms crossed. "Go on."

"Upon her death, we were named the legal guardians. Valerie's mother and I have been raising him for four years, even though my wife had already begun the initial stages of Alzheimer's. She now requires an attendant twenty-four hours a day. I've continued as best I can, but the doctors tell me I have to make a change. That's the only reason I'm here."

"A change?" Linc prodded.

"I have cancer. Damn thing is terminal," he growled. "I'll be gone within months."

Linc's face softened marginally, his anger at being excluded from his son's life still raging within him. He wanted to pull the old man from his chair, express his fury in a more physical way, but he managed to control his emotions.

"How did you find me?"

"I've always known where you were. I've tracked you from the time you married Valerie until now. I may be a cold-hearted S.O.B, but I'm not stupid. I figured you'd need to know about your son one day and didn't want to waste time finding you. Your trail is pretty hard to miss. A decorated SEAL turned successful businessman. You've done well for yourself." Douglas bent over, covering his mouth as a coughing fit shook his failing body.

Linc started toward him, then stopped when the man held up a hand. "Gets worse each day."

Pouring a glass of water, he held it out to Douglas. "I want to see him."

"But do you *want* him?"

Linc's jaw tightened, stopping a sharp and quite inappropriate response. "Yes. I want him. Now, where is he?"

******

Linc paced back and forth in the small meeting room, his stomach churning as Douglas arranged for his driver to return to TSR.

"What's his name?"

"Caiden Bergman Caldwell. Valerie had the good sense to acknowledge you as the father, which will simplify the legal issues."

"Then why wasn't I notified upon her death?"

"Connections, Caldwell. I lived my life building and developing them. A couple phone calls and Caiden was placed under my control." Bergman pulled out his phone and punched a number. "Yes, bring him in. I'll meet you in the lobby." He walked up to Linc, holding up his hand. "He knows I had to meet someone and that he may be moving to a new home. He does not know you're his father. Give me a few minutes with him." He searched Linc's face. "Please."

Linc nodded, his body humming in anticipation sprinkled with a dose of fear. He snorted at the realization. He'd felt fear a few times as a SEAL. Not once had anything in his civilian life triggered the same sense of alarm.

107

"I'll wait in my office. Have the receptionist call me when you're ready." Linc opened the door. "Be warned. I'll wait five minutes, then I'm coming for my son."

******

Grabbing a glass, Selena poured until the wine came to within an inch of the top. She took a sip, glancing again at the time. Seven o'clock, and still no word from Linc. If he hadn't been so consistent since their first night, his silence wouldn't concern her. Her own instincts telling her something bothered him also ratcheted up her anxiety. Selena mentally slapped herself, refusing to be one of those clingy, drama queen females who acted out whenever her man didn't act the way she expected.

Her man. Was he? Did he see himself as an important part of her life the way she did, or was this just another of his casual relationships? He seemed to excel at those.

She'd never said a word to him about the women who'd approached her over the last few weeks, giving her *friendly* advice, warning her not to get too comfortable. Seems the man had left a trail of broken hearts during his time in Peregrine Bay. Even her sister, Caly, had warned her to go slow. Although a gentleman and quite generous, he'd never shown the least bit of interest in extending any of his relationships beyond a few weeks. Selena wondered if she fell into the same category and he just hadn't gotten around to telling her.

Perhaps she could find out. Picking up her phone, she typed a short text, hovering over the message a few seconds before swallowing her fear and pressing *SEND*. Nothing to do now except wait.

******

"They're ready for you, Linc."

He wiped his sweaty hands down his pants at the receptionist's announcement and took a slow breath. "I'll be right there."

Standing, he shoved his fingers through his hair, not bothering to check the mirror behind one of the cabinet doors. As he headed toward the lobby, his phone vibrated. Retrieving it, he saw Selena's name and winced. Stopping abruptly, he debated on whether to text her back now or wait. He didn't want to leave her hanging.

Still at work. I'll call tomorrow.

Ever since leaving her bed, Linc had thought of her often, wishing he could do nothing more than slide under the covers and pull her into his arms. He felt a sense of relief at sending the message. At least she knew he was thinking about her.

Opening the door to the lobby, his gaze locked on a small boy playing on the floor. Several plastic figures were spread out around him, his hands moving from one to another.

Douglas turned toward him, nodding for Linc to go ahead.

Taking a deep breath, he walked toward his son, then crouched low, sitting on the floor a couple feet away. When Caiden looked up at him, his heart stopped. He had dark brown hair and striking blue eyes that seemed to miss nothing. His gaze darted to his grandfather, then back to Linc before focusing once more on the figures before him.

"I used to play with a set almost like this when I was your age. May I?" Linc indicated a soldier decked out in combat gear.

"Okay. That one is Buster."

"Buster, huh?" Linc picked up the figure, moving toward a tank a few inches away. "Which one do you have?"

"Linc. He's my favorite."

His throat tightened.

"My name is Caiden, but Grandpa says I can shorten it to Caid if I want. I like Caid better." He held up the camo-clad soldier. "This is the first one I got. Grandpa told me my mama had a friend named Linc, so that's his name." He set the soldier back on the floor, his gaze darting back to Linc. "What's your name?"

"I, uh…" He shot a look at Douglas.

"You know, I think I'll get some fresh air, Caiden. Perhaps you can stay in here and keep him company." Douglas indicated Linc with a nod. "I won't be gone long."

"Okay, Grandpa."

For ten minutes, neither said anything as they played with the figures, automatically becoming comrades against an unseen evil across the room.

"Grandpa says I have to live with someone else. That's why we came here." Caid didn't look up as he spoke, his voice signaling no emotion, as if changing homes was an everyday occurrence. He lifted a figure into the air, his gaze following it until his eyes locked on Linc. "Am I going to live with you?"

In all his years, Linc had never felt so out of his element. Leading a SEAL team battling insurgents? No problem. Running a multi-million dollar corporation with clients around the world? Piece of cake. Knowing the right words to say to his six-year-old son had him tied in knots.

"I'd very much like you to live with me, if that's what you want to do."

"Can we play with my men?" Caid nodded at the figures on the floor.

"Of course."

"Are there other kids?"

"No, but I'm sure we can find friends for you." He'd somehow find playmates for his son.

Minutes passed, neither saying anything. Linc watched his son make up his mind.

"Will you be my dad?" Caid slowly lifted his head, staring into Linc's eyes.

Linc felt his throat tighten. "Yes. I'll be your dad."

Without warning, Caid dropped the toy and launched himself at Linc, wrapping his small arms around his neck, holding tight. Burying his face in his son's hair, Linc fought back tears. He couldn't remember ever crying. Not over his short, failed marriage or the deaths of comrades. He'd held strong, keeping his emotions in check, showing no weakness. It stunned him how this one small child, his son, brought him to his knees.

Chapter Ten

Julia studied the documents before her. At Tom Harten's request, the meeting to decide who would provide security services for the arts center had been changed twice. She and the mayor had refused the councilman's third request, saying they could wait no longer.

"I'm sorry, Tom, but I simply do not see the significance of what you're telling us. You've provided anonymous reports of security failures at TSR client sites, yet you aren't able to confirm the breaches with any of their clients. Maybe if you could provide some validation, it would be easier to take these seriously." Julia couldn't take much more of Tom Harten's attempts to discredit Linc's firm. He needed to either give them solid evidence of TSR failing to provide agreed upon services, or get off his soapbox.

Tom opened his mouth to reply, but the mayor cut him off.

"I must agree with Julia. I'm glad you're working hard to find the best solution for security at the arts center. So far, I see nothing except conjecture and accusation. Have you spoken with the clients?" Mayor Timmons almost never saw issues the same way as Tom. Being the consummate politician, he always felt it right to give someone a gracious way out.

"Plus, I'd like to see similar reports on the other companies. Why are we just seeing those incidences on TSR and not on the other submitting company?" Herman Jost, the owner of the local jewelry store and member of the committee, sat back in his seat, crossing his arms. "This is a good idea, Tom. I think we need to expand the search to include Simondson Security. If I'm correct, the other two have both withdrawn."

"Yes, they have, Herman," Tom huffed out. He'd thought the data Ephraim Simondson had given him would be sufficient to shift Herman's view and, with any luck, the mayor's. Although a fixture in Peregrine Bay, winning every election over the last fifteen years, Timmons still kept his pulse on the voters and could be swayed if given enough contrary information to change his mind. Ephraim would need to dig deeper.

"I have another question for you, Tom. Simondson sent one of his employees, his stepson, Chad Donovan, to Peregrine Bay. I met with the young man this week. He mentioned you and he were friends in college." Timmons watched as Harten's jaw twitched. "Will this be a conflict for you?"

Tom stared at the mayor. Sitting back in his chair, he crossed his arms, focusing his attention on Julia. "No more of a conflict than Julia's sister dating Linc Caldwell. I believe that's much more of a conflict than my connection to Chad Donovan."

Julia didn't let her anger show. "I can assure you and the rest of this committee that my sister's personal life has no bearing on my recommendation and vote. Can you say the same, Tom?"

"Absolutely. It's been years since I've seen Chad. And to be accurate, my *brother* and Donovan were close friends. I met Chad through him."

Mayor Timmons glanced at the other committee members. "There are five of us on the committee. Recusing two might be unwise at this point. If you both can assure us your votes will be based solely on the merits of each company, I suggest we continue as we've been doing. Agreed?"

"I have no issue with it, Mayor," Herman Jost answered as the others nodded.

"Excellent. When do you think you can obtain what we need, Tom?" Julia hid the contempt she felt, although she had to concede that if he presented substantiated claims about either company, the findings would need to be considered–but only after significant vetting.

"Give me two weeks."

"We can't go any longer than that. The general contractor says once the foundation is poured, he needs to start working with the security firm. That is exactly two weeks away." The mayor gathered his papers and stood. "Unless there's other business, we're done."

Julia left the meeting, closing the conference door behind her, then taking the steps down to the sidewalk, glancing up at the darkening sky. She walked the short distance to her office, wondering if Selena had decided to work late. Julia knew she needed to speak with her about Chad, give her a heads-up about her college acquaintance being connected to Simondson, as well as Tom Harten.

She knew Selena held no animosity toward Chad, blaming herself for a lack of judgment in attending the party. Still, Julia didn't want her blindsided if Chad's company won the award or he attended a local function with Tom. As Jonathon said, you could never be too careful.

✱✱✱✱✱✱

"I can't do anymore until you give me some solid proof TSR failed to live up to client agreements." Tom balanced the phone against his ear as he sorted through the data Ephraim had sent to him.

"The fact there have been significant attempts to breach their system isn't enough?" Ephraim barked. He wasn't used to losing business, especially not to a firm still getting their feet wet in the security business. No amount of digging had uncovered how TSR had won so many awards and grown so much in such a short time. Ephraim felt certain their success had more to do with connections and kickbacks than competence and experience, yet he'd found nothing to confirm his suspicions.

"No, it's not. In fact, they want me to prepare a similar report on Simondson Security." Tom cringed at the expletives coming from the other end of the line. "You can't expect anything else, Ephraim. You and TSR are the final two bidders. They want all the data on each firm, not just accusations directed at Caldwell's company."

"I'm paying you significant money to help us on this, Tom." Ephraim let the implied threat settle between them.

"Reelection is tricky for a politician suspected of taking bribes."

Tom swallowed the ball of fire in his throat, feeling the sweat build on his brow. He wished he'd never connected with Ephraim or reconnected with his stepson, Chad. In college, Tom's brother and Chad had been close friends, traveling to California after graduation and finding an apartment. Although the three had hung out together a few times, Tom had never been close to Chad.

"Threaten me all you want, Ephraim. It doesn't change the fact that if I go down, so will you and your entire company," Tom hissed, tired of feeling bullied. "You didn't pay me enough to take the fall alone." He hung up. Ephraim would either send him more data on TSR or he wouldn't. Tom didn't care. He'd deposited the large amount of cash in an account no one could trace, which meant they could never prove he took a cent. A self-satisfied grin crossed his face as he thought of how he'd spend all that money.

******

Selena woke early Sunday morning. She'd had a rough night, falling asleep well after midnight, then tossing and turning until sunrise. Day five and still no word from Linc since his brief text saying he'd call her. He never did.

Rolling out of bed, her shoulders slumped as she walked to the kitchen for coffee. While the cup filled, she checked her messages. Nothing. Letting out a deep sigh, Selena stirred creamer into her coffee, tossing the spoon into the sink. Settling on the sofa, she absently surfed through various television channels, then turned it off in frustration.

She refused to mourn what appeared to be the end of the brief relationship. No matter how much he'd meant to her, it had become obvious she couldn't be further from his mind. If he were hurt or sick, either Matt or Shane would call to let her know. There could be just one reason he'd fallen out of touch, and the thought brought a sharp pain to her chest. For the first time, she began to understand how Julia must have felt all those years ago when Adam walked away after years as a couple. At least Selena only had to deal with the pain of weeks.

Pushing off the sofa, she scrambled to grab her ringing phone, checking the caller ID. Disappointment surrounded her when she saw Caly's name.

"Good morning, Caly. Thanks for dinner last night." Selena worked to put a happy tone in her voice.

"Still no word from your boy, huh?"

"I didn't say that," Selena snapped.

"You didn't have to, sweetie. What are you doing today, besides going to Father's for dinner?"

"Honestly, I hadn't thought about it. Linc usually plans our Sundays." She paused, realizing how much she'd come to depend on him in such a short period of time. Fishing, hiking, kayaking, or car trips ending in a picnic in some remote spot.

"He could still call. You know that hostage situation in Indonesia last week?"

Selena's brows drew together. "Vaguely. What does that have to do with Linc?"

"Caro Systems is one of his clients. I'll bet he was up for a couple days and nights dealing with that mess. At least he never had to take over the rescue operation. Seems the police messed it up all on their own."

"How do you know all this?"

"Because I keep up with online reports, unlike some of us who hunker down when she walks through the front door."

"Funny," Selena countered, although the comment didn't strike her as humorous. "I mean, how do you know TSR was involved?"

"I have my sources. Truthfully, I'd planned to ask you about it last night, but between your foul temper and my canceled date, neither of us were in the mood for much conversation. Anyway, how about going with me to Pine Cove? There are a couple boutiques I've wanted to visit. We could shop, grab lunch, then take a trip around the east side of the lake. We'll get to Father's in plenty of time for dinner."

Selena's mind still worked to process the fact TSR and Linc may have been involved in the executive kidnapping. If so, perhaps he'd simply been too busy to call…or text.

Who was she kidding? The man could talk, text, and prepare a client presentation all at the same time. If he had the slightest inclination, sending her one small text would've taken him ten seconds.

"Selena? You still there?" Caly's voice carried through the phone, shaking Selena from her depressing thoughts.

"Yes, I'm here."

"So what about it?"

"Can we stop by Linc's house? I'd like to drop some things off for him."

"Are you sure you want to do that? It's been less than a week, and from what I've heard, he must have been consumed with resolving the client issue. You may want to give him a few more days." Caly's voice had grown serious and thick with concern.

Selena let out a deep sigh. "I know you mean well, and it could be great advice. The thing is, I need to protect myself. Even returning the few items he's left here doesn't have to signal the end."

"I'm pretty certain that's *exactly* what he'll believe."

Selena ignored Caly, focusing on what she believed to be right. "And he'll probably be relieved I got the hint without him having to spell it out. I'll go with you, but only if you stop at his place."

"Fine. It's your life. Be ready at ten."

Selena set her phone on the counter, then looked around the house she'd fixed up on a meager budget. It still showed its age, even though huge improvements had been made. She shook her head, making her way to a bookcase where two of Linc's books sat.

He'd never hesitated to answer when asked about the women in his life. Before her, he'd dated mostly well-known, sophisticated women with wealth and homes so large, three of hers could fit inside. Even though her father had money, he'd always encouraged his daughters to make it on their own. She, along with Julia and Caly, had succeeded, and Selena had no doubt their two younger sisters, Danielle and Lillian, would do the same. Even so, her accomplishments were no match for the women who flitted in and out of Linc's life for years.

Grabbing a box from the garage, she put the two books in it, then continued through the house, adding a pullover sweater, a pair of jeans, two t-shirts, a toothbrush, and a comb. The nightstand on the side of the bed where he usually slept held a few coins and one of his pens. She swept them into the box, then took one more turn around the room, seeing nothing else.

Setting the box on her bed, she pulled a pair of pants and a blouse from the closet, then stepped into the shower. Letting the hot water slide over her body, she felt a sharp pang of regret. She hoped Caly wasn't right about her reacting too quickly to his lack of communication. Being truthful with herself, Selena knew her fear of being the last one to know he'd moved on pushed her to close the loop with Linc. She absolutely did not want to walk into a restaurant one night to see him with someone else. Better to be proactive than reactive. She snickered, remembering the times Linc had said the same to her. They hadn't been together long, yet she felt she'd learned so much from him. Most of all, she'd reclaimed her confidence and belief in her ability to attract a man. As much as she ached at the thought of never being with him again, she couldn't help but thank him for the most amazing few weeks of her life.

Chapter Eleven

"I love this shop, Caly." Selena picked up another handmade scarf, wrapping it around her neck. "This goes perfect with this blouse. And these earrings are gorgeous."

"So buy them. You can wear them tonight at dinner." Caly held up a short silk dress with bright colors and an outrageous design. "What do you think?"

"It's definitely you," Selena responded, acknowledging the extreme differences between Caly and her. Outspoken and free-spirited, their father told them she was much like her mother, Breeze, who'd died shortly after Calypso's birth. "Where do you plan to wear it?"

"Anywhere. Everywhere," she laughed, snatching up a bright orange purse to match the most prominent color in the dress.

Waiting for the clerk to ring up and bag their purchases, Selena turned toward Caly. "I'm so glad you convinced me to come to Pine Cove before stopping by Linc's. I needed a little boost before dropping off his things."

Caly placed a hand on Selena's arm. "Are you certain you want to do this? I'm no expert on relationships, but I swear that man is crazy about you. Is it too much to take a step back and wait a few more days?"

She'd been thinking the same, but after checking her phone four times over the last two hours and seeing nothing, she'd realized accepting he'd moved on was her only choice.

"I'm certain. If he's home, I'll do it in a way that leaves the door open. If he's not, I'll just leave the box and let it speak for itself." Picking up her items, she walked toward the door. "Come on. Let's get this over with."

******

"Last chance to turn around and head home," Caly said as she pulled to a stop outside Linc's gated entry.

"Nope. I've made up my mind." Selena got out, punched in the security code, then slipped back into the car as the gate opened. "Park over there." She pointed to an open area not far from the front doors. Retrieving the box from the trunk, she straightened her blouse and her shoulders, determined to do this in as gracious a manner as possible.

Although she had the code for the gate, she'd never asked for the code to the front door—and he'd never offered. Which made sense since he didn't have a key to her place. Pushing down the last vestiges of fear, feeling her heart squeeze, she knocked. One massive door opened almost instantly, a large man with broad shoulders and huge muscles staring at her. From Linc's description, she thought this must be Brut.

"Can I help you?" He stuck his head out the door and looked around.

"I'm Selena Kerrigan. You must be Brut."

"Yes, ma'am. What can I do for you?" Neither the fact she knew his name nor the mention of hers had any impact on him.

"I, um…wanted to drop this off for Linc. Is he here?"

"Yes, ma'am. He's out by the lake, entertaining someone. Do you want to wait on the patio?" He gestured through the house. She glanced around him to see a woman standing on the patio, then taking the steps to the backyard. Slim and tall with a stunning figure, the woman's long black hair cascaded down her back.

Sucking in an agonized breath, Selena braced herself, accepting he did have a new woman in his life. He'd moved on without giving her a thought. The fact her instincts had been right provided no comfort.

Looking at the box in her hand, logical thought fled as her heart sank. "If it's all right, I'll leave this with you." She held out the box, feeling a sense of loss when Brut took it from her hands.

He looked at it, then glanced behind him. "You sure you don't want to give it to the boss yourself?"

"Quite certain. Thank you, Brut." She quickly turned, dashing for the car before the full impact of her action hit her. Jumping inside, she glanced at Caly, tears blurring her vision. "Let's get out of here."

"Oh, honey, are you all right?"

"No, I'm not all right. Please, let's just go." Selena buried her face in her hands, sobs marring her normally serene face.

Caly drove through the gate and up the winding road toward the main highway. Pulling over into a large vacant lot, she killed the engine and reached over to wrap her arms around Selena. Saying nothing, she held tight, letting her sister cry until there were no more tears. Pulling back, she reached behind her, grabbing a tissue from a box on the floor.

"Here. Take this."

Selena snatched it from her hand. "I'll need more than one."

Caly handed her a few more, then sat back. "What did he say?"

"He didn't say anything. A man named Brut opened the door. He told me Linc was in the back yard, entertaining someone. I saw her, Caly…the woman he's now seeing." Tears threatened again. This time, she closed her eyes tight, refusing to let them fall. "I suspected as much when I didn't hear from him." She sniffed a few more times, then dried her eyes. "We can go now. I'll be fine." Although she tried to sound confident, Selena knew she would not be fine for a long time.

******

"Daddy, stop. I can't breathe." Caid rolled on the grass, his giggles spreading across the massive backyard. Linc stopped tickling him and sat back.

"Next time, think about who you shoot your squirt gun at." Linc smiled at his son, warmth wrapping around him from the little boy who'd already claimed his heart.

Caid jumped up, ran behind Linc, and grabbed the small red plastic toy he'd been given. He started squirting his father again, then ran, his short legs carrying him to the back

126

patio, where he hid behind a large potted plant. "Got you. Got you." He peeked around the plant, but didn't see Linc. A cold blast of water soaked his back and had him squealing before he took off down the steps to the lawn.

Linc laughed, holding his stomach. The last few days had been a whirlwind. He'd applied for legal guardianship, flown with Caid to Douglas's house to pack the rest of his son's belongings, visited his parents and introduced them to their grandson, then flown home. He'd already hired a nanny, knowing he'd need help, and enrolled Caid in school. In between all of that, he'd talked with Matt or Shane a few times about minor business issues, spending as much time as possible getting to know his son.

"Thought you might want this, boss."

Linc turned to grab the two towels Brut held out. "Thanks."

"Some lady came by about half an hour ago and left a box for you."

He stopped wiping his face and looked up. "Did she leave her name?"

"Selma? No, that's not it."

"Selena?" Linc asked, turning to look through the windows toward the front doors.

"Yeah, that's it. Selena."

Linc turned toward the nanny, who'd started the day before. "Nina, please watch Caid for me."

"Of course, Mr. Caldwell."

Dropping the towels, he dashed through the house to pick up the box. Tearing off the tape, his breath caught when he saw the contents. Mumbling a curse, he glanced through the items, then dropped the box to pull his phone from his pocket.

"Come on, Selena. Pick up," he whispered to himself as the call went to voicemail. "Selena, it's Linc. I just got the box. What the h…" He heard little footsteps running up behind him, "heck is going on? Call me." He set the phone aside as Caid stopped beside him.

"Can we go fishing now?" His face brightened as he jumped up and down.

Linc looked down at his son, placing a hand on his head and ruffling the silky brown hair. "Sure, son. Just give me a few minutes. Brut, would you mind getting the fishing gear together?"

"No problem, boss. Come on, squirt. You can help me." Brut headed for a large storage building around back, Caid running at his side.

"I'll pack a lunch for you and Caid, Mr. Caldwell," Nina offered, turning toward the kitchen.

"Thanks, Nina." He watched her walk from the room, mentally thanking Matt for suggesting her. She'd responded right away, fitting seamlessly into the routine with little effort.

Linc and Caid had taken to each other immediately, almost as if they'd been together the last six years. He'd been so busy, consumed with getting everything right with his son, he'd pushed everything else aside, including Selena.

"Ah, hell." He pushed fingers through his damp hair. It had been almost a week since he'd last seen her. He'd meant to call several times, but it had been close to midnight by the time he fell into bed each night, then Caid would wake him at five each morning, clamoring for his attention. The days had been so full, he hardly had time to take a deep breath. Thank goodness Matt and Shane knew the situation and told him to get lost for a couple weeks.

He glanced at the box as a slow ache tightened his chest, wondering what he had been thinking. She should have been one of the first people he called about Caid. Instead, he'd immersed himself into learning to be a father, preparing for life with his son. Now he had to deal with the possible loss of the woman he suspected had already captured his heart.

Adam had been right. He should've told Selena about Valerie when he had the chance. If he had, the news about Caid wouldn't be so hard to explain.

Picking up the box, Linc headed for his bedroom, dumping the contents on the bed. Not much, but he wanted them right where they were—in her house. A sense of peace washed over him when he thought of Selena's inviting, comfortable home. Relaxing there had been the best part of each day they were together. Looking around his massive bedroom, he felt a chill pass through him. It was just a place to live, not a home.

His gaze moved to his dresser, landing on a hair brush, one of those stretchy bands next to it. No woman had ever left anything at his house. He didn't allow it. Until Selena. Feeling a ball of ice grow in his gut, he walked to the entry and picked up his phone. No message and no voicemail. Cursing again at his sheer stupidity, he called once more, leaving an almost identical message to his previous one, adding how sorry he was he hadn't called before. All he could do now was wait and hope she responded. If she didn't, he'd go after her. There was no way he'd let her walk away so easily.

******

Selena followed Caly into the Kerrigan home, not wanting to face her family—especially Julia and Adam. She wanted to plaster on a brave face, the same as other women who had brief affairs that ended too soon, but found the task too much of an effort. They'd been together a few short weeks, yet it seemed as if she'd known him forever. Her heart certainly felt like it.

"There you two are." Julia came to an abrupt stop when she focused on her sisters' faces. "What's wrong?"

"She and Linc split up." Caly glanced behind Julia toward the kitchen. "I need a glass of wine. Selena, do you want anything?"

Shaking her head, Selena started to move past Julia, only to have her sister grasp her arm.

"What happened?"

"It's not a big deal. He met someone else and moved on. And before you ask, yes, I'm fine with it."

"Come with me." Julia turned her toward their father's study, closing the door behind them. "Don't tell me you're fine because I can see from your face you're not. He never called?"

Selena took a shuddering breath, clasping her hands in front of her. "No word from him at all. A week with no calls or texts. Nothing. It didn't take a genius to realize what was happening, so I packed the few things he left at my house and dropped them off. He was *entertaining* his new lady."

"Tell me you did not walk in to find them together."

"No, nothing like that. I saw her when one of his employees took the box from me. I never did see Linc." Selena lowered herself into a nearby chair.

Julia took a seat next to her, grabbing her hand. "So you didn't talk to him, ask what was going on?"

"Well, no."

"Has he called since you dropped off the box?"

Shaking her head, Selena pulled the phone from her purse and turned it on. "I shut it off." Waiting while it powered up, she leaned back in the overstuffed chair. "At this point, his excuses don't interest me." Her eyes narrowed when she saw two voice messages, both from Linc.

"Did he call?" Julia prodded.

"Yes." Selena slipped the phone back into her purse, not having the desire to listen to them now.

"You're not going to listen to what he has to say? What if you made a mistake and the woman isn't who you think?"

"And what if she is? I just don't want to deal with it right now. Later, but not now." Standing, Selena took purposeful strides out of the room, leaving Julia to stare at her retreating back.

******

Linc guided the twenty-foot fishing boat into an area known as a favorite for Lake Bountiful's trout population. Looking behind him, he smiled. Secured in his life vest, Caid held onto one of the metal railings, his hair blowing in the slight breeze, a huge smile on his face.

"Dad, when can we fish?" Caid let go of the railing, moving closer to Linc.

He couldn't suppress the joy he felt at Caid's use of the word *dad*. Never would he have thought one word could trigger so much emotion.

"A few more minutes and we'll be at my favorite spot on the lake." Linc's free arm snaked around his son's waist, holding him steady as he made a slow turn. "Can you wait that long?"

Caid nodded, his gaze following the direction of the boat, his small form vibrating with excitement. Linc slowed the engine and reached behind him, grabbing a short rod and reel rigged for a child. Tying on a hook and adding bait, he checked it over once more.

"Now?" Caid bounced on the balls of his feet, glancing from the rod to his father.

"Do you know how to cast?"

He shook his head, his face scrunching. "Uh-uh."

"It's okay. I'll do it, then you can catch the fish." Linc stepped to the other side of the boat, cast the line out, then reeled it in a little before handing it to Caid. "There you go."

Caid flashed him a brilliant smile. The punch to his gut was the same sensation he felt when Selena did the same.

Shoving his hands in his pockets, he watched Caid, his mind thinking about Selena. Three hours had passed since he left his second voicemail, but he already felt a sickening dread flow through his body. She'd always answered his messages within minutes. He wondered where she'd be on a late Sunday afternoon, then grimaced, remembering the invitation to her father's for dinner. As if on cue, his phone vibrated. He grabbed it, looking at the screen to see a text from Adam.

Adam: *What the hell's going on with you and Selena?*

Linc: *I screwed up. Is she at her father's?*

Adam: *Yeah, she's here. Can you make it?*

Linc: *Can't today. I'll explain when I see you.*

Adam: *Don't explain to me. Explain to Selena. Whatever's going on isn't working for her. Gotta go.*

Linc shoved the phone back into his pocket, considering his options. Caid started school tomorrow. He'd get him settled in class, swing by Selena's house, then her office. Somehow, he'd get her to listen to him. Hopefully, she'd understand about his past, as well as Caid. He cared too much to let her disappear from his life.

Within a few short days, his son had become his first priority. He vowed to work hard at being a father worthy of Caid's trust. Yet as hard as he tried, he also couldn't envision a future without Selena. He needed them both.

Chapter Twelve

"Ephraim, there isn't anything else I can give you. I know you don't want to hear it, but TSR is clean. Their clients are extremely loyal."

He could hear the frustration in the voice of the Simondson employee he'd sent to Peregrine Bay with orders to forward information on TSR client issues, breaches, and failures. So far, all Ephraim had received was a few deflected cyber-attacks and a botched hostage rescue operation that went against the recommendation of TSR. Nothing he could use to color the opinion of the city council.

"Then you'll need to create something," he growled.

"You want me to fabricate incidences where none exist? That's insane, Ephraim. They check and double check all client communication. I'm not good enough to hide that type of sabotage."

Sabotage, Ephraim pondered. He hadn't considered creating chaos within the company, certain they'd be able to uncover business improprieties or mismanagement. Perhaps his thinking had been too narrow. System shutdowns, cyber-attacks targeted at TSR, could be a better method to undermine their pristine record than sorting through benign hacking instances with little impact.

"Sabotage is an excellent idea and can be accomplished within hours—"

"No, it can't. You have no idea what you're asking or what goes into the type of actions you're considering. I'm not the person to do it."

"I didn't send you to Peregrine Bay to tell me what you *can't* do. You owe me."

His employee sighed. The hope of being able to build a life in Peregrine Bay had disintegrated into a war of wills with a man who held aspirations beyond reason. He'd built a successful business, which grew by over twenty percent each year. Still, it wasn't enough for him.

"You do not want to stoop to the actions you're requesting. Back away and let TSR have the arts center project. One lost contract is nothing compared to the backlash a botched sabotage attempt could cause."

"Then don't botch it," Ephraim hissed. "Do I need to itemize all the ways I've helped you over the years, the money I've thrown at your education, or the messes you've avoided because of me?"

"No, you don't."

"Then get to work on this. I need a significant event to occur before the committee makes its decision. Am I clear?"

"Yes, Ephraim, you are."

Slamming down the phone, Ephraim leaned back in his chair, crossing his arms. He never should've married a woman who dragged a kid along with her. No matter the money he provided over the years, the situation never changed—until he'd washed his hands of his wife's child. Recent circumstances required him to get more involved, but he'd exacted a price this time. No more free rides. Ephraim wanted something in return, and he'd get it.

******

Rolling to her side, Selena glanced at the clock, then jumped out of bed. Eight o'clock. She'd meant to be in the office by seven Monday morning, get an early start, fill her day with work, and start forgetting about Linc.

Taking a quick shower, she towel dried her hair, hearing a pounding on her front door. Slipping into sweats and a cotton camisole, she plodded through the living room, pulling open the door, then freezing at who stood outside.

"Thanks for finally answering." Linc didn't bother to hide the sarcasm. His scowl faltered when he got a good look at her, his mouth going dry. Damp hair, skin glistening from her shower, and tight top over lightweight pants which hugged her hips. "May I come in?" His voice dropped an octave.

"Yes. I mean, no."

"Well, which is it, Selena? Are you going to let me in so we can talk about what's going on, or are you going to make me shadow you until I break your defenses?"

She ran fingers through her hair, then crossed her arms, her chin jutting out. "I don't even know why you're here. Most men wouldn't be knocking on another woman's door when they have a girlfriend waiting for them at home."

Linc's jaw dropped. Of all the mistakes he'd made, hiding a girlfriend at his house wasn't one of them. "Girlfriend? What the hell are you talking about?"

Sending him a withering glare, she moved to close the door. "Forget it." Before it slammed shut, Linc inserted his booted foot and held out a firm arm.

"No, I won't forget it. You accused me of hiding a girlfriend at my place, which is a bunch of…which isn't true. The only girlfriend I have is you. Obviously, I somehow messed that up."

He saw the expression on her face change from defiance to confusion, her shoulders slumping.

"You get five minutes before I have to change for work." She opened the door enough to allow him to enter. "Don't waste the time."

Linc almost laughed at her bravado. Even with her fierce façade, he could see the redness in her eyes and the puffiness around them, both signs of little or no sleep. He may not have known her long, and she had never said the words, but he'd bet his life she'd fallen in love with him.

Moving close to touch her, she stepped aside, taking quick strides around the kitchen island and to the coffee pot. Pouring a cup for him and one for her, she carried them to the living room, holding one out.

"Okay, your time starts now."

He took the cup, taking a sip, refusing to sit until she did. With a raised brow, Selena sighed, lowering herself onto one end of the sofa. Linc took a seat next to her, scooting over until only inches separated them.

"Before I explain why I was out of touch, plead mea culpa, and beg your forgiveness, I want to know what you mean by my *girlfriend*."

She turned to face him. "You know, a female you're close to, one who stays at your house, a woman you entertain. The lady with whom you're currently sleeping." Her voice rose a notch with each phrase, red coloring her cheeks.

"And you're implying that woman isn't you?" He studied her face, trying to understand what she was telling him.

"Stop it, Linc. I saw her at your house. Long black hair, slim, attractive. Does that ring a bell?"

It took him a minute before his face shifted from confusion to amusement. "Jealous?"

Jumping up, she stomped a few feet away, then turned with her hands on her hips. "You think this is funny?"

Standing, Linc held his hands out in front of him, palms out. "No, darlin', I don't think it's funny at all."

"Then you admit she exists?" Her voice faltered, the color draining from her face.

"C'mere, Selena."

"No. Not until I understand why you couldn't tell me about her. Why I had to stumble onto your secret."

Scrubbing a hand down his face, he let his arms fall to his sides. "You stumbled onto a secret all right, but the nanny is just one part of it."

Her eyes widened and breath hitched. "Nanny?"

He took slow steps toward her, allowing her to push him away if she wanted. When she didn't, he wrapped his arms around her, pulling her close.

"I have a lot to tell you and none of it involves a girlfriend, unless we mean you." He kissed her temple, then swept her into his arms. Taking a seat on a nearby chair, he settled her on his lap, a sense of relief washing over him when she wrapped her arms around his neck.

"That's better. Now, let me tell you about my week."

******

"Married? But you said you'd never been in love." She pulled away to look at him. "Why didn't you tell me?"

He closed his eyes, remembering Adam's advice. "The relationship wasn't love, Selena, but lust. I'm not proud of the fact, but it's the truth. I was married for a few short months. We were together a total of three weeks before my team got orders to ship out. By the time I returned home, the annulment had been finalized." He swiped an errant strand of hair from her face. "Honestly, I never thought about her after that, barely remembered I'd ever been married. It had become a non-event for me."

She mulled this over, trying to decide what to make of the fact he'd been less than honest. "I don't understand why you didn't just tell me. Why would you hide it?"

"As I recall, you asked if I'd ever been in love. I answered honestly. You're right, though. I should've told you, and would have, except it just didn't seem important.

139

Few people even know about the brief relationship and no one ever talks about it." He brushed a kiss across her forehead, feeling fortunate she didn't pull away.

"All right. I can somewhat understand, but what does that have to do with the fact you disappeared from my life?"

"Believe me, I didn't mean to disappear." Linc kissed her lips, then slid her off his lap and stood, pacing to the window. The wind had picked up, causing even the tallest pines to sway. Taking a deep breath, he turned toward her. "Last week, I learned something *had* come from my brief marriage."

Sitting with her legs crossed, hands clasped in her lap, she shook her head. "What?"

"I have a son, Selena." He let the words sink in, seeing her eyes go wide, her lips part.

"My God…" A hand came up to cover her mouth as she absorbed the news.

"Yeah." Shoving his hands in his pockets, he turned back toward the window, watching the wind create patterns as it swirled around the branches, lifting heavy limbs, then letting them fall. "His name is Caiden and he's six." Linc could feel a smile tug at the corners of his mouth as he spun back toward her. "Caid's a part of my life now. I won't turn my back on him." His expression held a hint of defiance, a challenge for her to disagree.

Selena pushed up, walking to him with outstretched arms. Wrapping them around his waist, she nuzzled his neck, taking in the familiar scent that was completely Linc.

"Why would you even think of not being there for him?" she whispered.

Linc could feel his body relax as he pulled her closer, resting his chin on the top of her head. "Valerie never told me about him. When she died a few years ago, her parents became Caiden's legal guardians. His grandmother has Alzheimer's, and his grandfather's been diagnosed with terminal cancer. If it hadn't been for circumstances, I may have gone to my grave never knowing." The familiar feel of fury began to burn, then died out as Selena held him tighter. Her touch calmed him, brought him back to a place where he felt at peace.

She glanced up, her eyes moist. "You are going to make the most amazing father."

"You think so?"

"I know so, Lincoln Caldwell. Any little boy, or girl, would be very fortunate to call you... What *does* he call you?"

"Dad, or sometimes Daddy." Linc almost choked on the emotions that slammed into him. Clearing his throat, he looked at her. "And what would you call me, Selena?"

She grinned against his chest. "My boyfriend?"

"Good girl." He dropped his arms, taking a step back. "Caid's in school until three o'clock. Would you like to come over to my place after work and have dinner with us?"

A smile broke out across her face, the same one that always punched him in his belly.

"I'd like that very much."

"That's good," he breathed out. Letting a finger trail down her cheek, he leaned in, taking her mouth with his. It had been almost a full week since he'd felt her soft body against him. He didn't know the protocol for sleeping with his woman while his son slept in a room next door, but he'd bet it wasn't a good idea. At least not yet. "When do you have to be at work?"

Her mind fogged, feeling his lips doing funny things as they trailed a path down her neck, then toward the swell of her breasts. At the moment, she couldn't think of a single reason she had to be at the office anytime soon.

"I'll take your silence as permission to stay and pick up where we left off last week." Bending, he lifted her into his arms, then walked to her bedroom, kicking the door shut. He didn't plan to let her go until the school bell rang.

******

"Hey, C. Haven't heard from you in forever. Where you been keeping yourself." Phone to his ear, Rave sat back in his chair, giving his eyes a rest from their constant vigilance on the computer screen.

"Around. Right now, I'm in a hick town near Lake Bountiful in Idaho, trying to do a job for my stepfather."

"Yeah? And what would that be?"

"That's why I called you, Rave. The old man is hanging all the old crap over my head. This time, he's ordering me to make something happen with one of his competitors. It's completely out of my league."

"I'm guessing it has to do with busting into a system, or..." His voice trailed off as he thought through the possibilities.

"Any type of disruption that'll damage their reputation. The issue is time."

"Let me guess, C. He wants it done yesterday."

"Of course he does. That's how the man rolls."

"Why do you still let him push you around? You've been on your own long enough to cut ties with the man, unless there are things you've never mentioned."

"It's my mother. He still controls the purse strings, so she'll be the one to suffer if I don't do what he asks. Every time I get myself straight, he yanks on the leash, screwing up all my plans. Look, I'll understand if you don't want to help out. There's a risk on this one."

"What's the risk?" Rave asked, his interest piqued.

"The target is Templar Security & Rescue."

"TSR?" He let out a couple choice expletives, then took a breath. "Is the old man nuts? They have some of the best equipment and brain power in the business. Word on the street is they're expensive, but their record is pristine. Client's line up to work with them."

"Yeah, I've already learned that. Hey, I had to ask. Thanks anyway—"

"Hold on, C. I never said I wouldn't help."

"If you're certain. We don't need anything pointing back to us, Rave."

"I have a couple ideas. Send me all the specifics, including Ephraim's deadline. I'll set something up and get back to you. You never know. I might be the one to blow TSR's unblemished record."

"Thanks, Rave. I owe you."

Chapter Thirteen

"Daddy, Brut says to tell you someone is at the door." Caid crooked his finger at Linc, signaling him to bend low so he could whisper in his ear. "It's a girl." His eyes grew wide when a grin appeared on his father's face.

Linc kept his voice low, as if they were sharing an important secret. "Wow. A girl, huh? Guess we should go check this out."

Caid's head bobbed up and down. "Come on." He took off running, stopping in the foyer, then looked over his shoulder. Linc stood right behind him, his gaze riveted on the woman he'd made love to most of the day, until fatherly duties called.

Brut nodded at Linc, then Selena, before disappearing down a long hall.

Walking to her, Linc slid an arm around her waist, pulling her close, kissing her cheek.

"Selena, I'd like you to meet my son, Caiden. Caid, this is my very good friend, Ms. Kerrigan."

Caid stood still, arms at his side, his mouth open. A few seconds passed before Selena walked toward him, bending down and extending her hand.

"Hello, Caiden. It's a pleasure to meet you. I'd like it if you would call me Selena."

Anxious eyes glanced at his father, then back to Selena before he held out his hand. "I like to be called Caid."

"Then that's what I'll call you. I hope we can be good friends."

Linc held his breath, watching the interaction between the two most important people in his life. The magnitude of Caid's acceptance of Selena crashed into him. Until this moment, he hadn't acknowledged how much he wanted his son to accept her.

"Okay." Caid's grin turned mischievous as he cast a look at Linc. "Can she fish?"

Linc couldn't contain the chuckle or the relief on his face. "I do believe she can. Perhaps we'll go out on the lake this weekend and test her skills."

Caid gave a solemn nod, his face scrunched and lips pursed as if preparing to make an important announcement. His gaze turned to Selena. "You can't wear a dress on the boat. Right, Dad?"

"Very true. Pants, shirt, tennis shoes, and a hat are standard issue for boarding my ship."

"Want to come see my new pole?" Caid held his hand out to Selena, tugging her after him.

"I guess I'll see you in a little bit," she smiled, glancing over her shoulder at Linc.

Nodding, he swallowed the lump in his throat. *This could be my life*, he thought. Two weeks ago, the notion of making a commitment to one woman and becoming a father would have sounded insane. Today, watching his son dash away with Selena in tow, he couldn't imagine anything he wanted more.

******

Selena stood next to Caid, listening as he instructed her on the fine points of casting a fishing line. His similarities to Linc were obvious. The way his eyes moved, the expressiveness and serious manner were so much like his father, she found herself paying more attention to his voice and actions rather than the words.

"You want to try?" Caid held the pole out to her.

"If you're certain I won't break it."

"Naw. My dad says it's indes…indes…"

"Indestructible?" Selena prompted.

"That's it. He says it would be pretty hard to break. If I get a big fish, I have to hold tight or he'll swim away with it." His lips drew into a thin line.

Selena plastered on a solemn expression to match his. "I don't believe that will be a problem, Caid. You're big and strong. Much stronger than any of the fish I've seen in Lake Bountiful."

He beamed up at her, then turned toward the house when he heard the patio door close.

"There's my dad."

Shielding her eyes from the late evening sun, she placed the other hand on her stomach in an effort to control the butterflies bursting within her. Her reaction to him never changed. Even when he'd stood at her door this morning, her heart squeezing in intense pain at what she thought had happened, she still wanted him. Feelings of anger and betrayal tended to slip away when he stood so near. It had taken all her willpower to keep her distance. The words he'd said before leaving to pick up Caid at school still rang in her ears.

"We will never again jump to conclusions. Agreed?" When she had nodded, he'd lifted her chin with his finger, leaving her with the feel of his soft, caressing kiss. She'd stood at the door several minutes after he left, not wanting to break the warmth of their time together.

"What are you staring at, sweetheart?" He wrapped an arm around her, drawing her close, tilting his head toward her ear. "You couldn't be thinking of how we spent most of our day, could you?" His smug smile was all too knowing.

"I have no idea what you're referring to, Mr. Caldwell." The deep blush belied her response.

"Did you see me cast?" Caid's undisguised energy drew Linc's attention.

"Later," he whispered before dropping his arm and turning toward his son. "I did see you. Were you able to teach Selena all our tricks?"

"She didn't try yet. Maybe you can help her."

Linc glanced at Selena, his eyes sparkling. They'd fished several times and he'd learned she could teach him more about catching fish on Lake Bountiful than the other way around.

"Yes, Linc. Maybe you can help the uninitiated female." She crossed her arms, her voice full of humor.

"Well, I—"

"Mr. Caldwell, I'm going to leave now, unless you need me to help more with Caid."

Selena turned to see the woman who'd caught her attention the previous day standing on the patio.

"Come on, Selena. Let me introduce you to Caid's nanny."

She set the rod and reel on a nearby chair as Linc grabbed her hand, then Caid's, and walked toward the house.

"Selena, this is Nina Trahant, Caid's nanny.

Selena stepped forward. "It's a pleasure to meet you, Ms. Trahant."

"Please, call me Nina." She accepted the outstretched hand, placing her other hand on top in a welcoming gesture. "Mr. Caldwell has spoken of you." When her eyes crinkled at the corners, Selena realized the beautiful woman was much older than she'd first thought. "All good things," she added, pulling her hand from Selena's.

"I'm still amazed at how quickly you were able to start. I know Linc is very grateful for your help." She glanced at Linc, hoping she hadn't overstepped.

"It all worked out as it should," Nina explained. "My husband passed away a year ago. After I took care of selling his business, it seemed my days were no longer full. This opportunity came at the perfect time."

"Shane got her name from one of our employees. Nina used to run a preschool, then retired when her husband's business took off. We're lucky to have her." Linc looked down at Caid, who'd already grown attached to the woman.

"Well, I'll be on my way." She glanced at Caid. "I have some ideas for after school tomorrow."

"You do. What?"

Caid slid his hand into Nina's as she nodded at Linc and Selena, then walked into the house, her voice trailing off. "Well, my grandfather was a great Shoshone warrior. Perhaps…"

Selena leaned into Linc. "She seems wonderful."

"So far. I never like to count too much on anything until I've had some time to study it. Her references were excellent and the fact her niece works for us played in her favor." Wrapping an arm around Selena's shoulders, he guided her into the house. "I hope you don't mind casual. Caid asked for spaghetti with meatballs."

"Sounds perfect."

Linc studied her face, thinking she was the one who was perfect.

******

"All right, big guy. It's time for bed." Linc and Selena finished the dishes while Caid finished the last of his homework at the kitchen counter. "Six years old and already doing homework," he muttered.

"Welcome to the realities of elementary school and daddyhood." She laughed, draping a towel on a hook. "You may want to have Nina work with him before you get home."

"Can I watch a movie?" Caid pleaded, his mouth turning to a slight pout.

"He's already working me," Linc mumbled under his breath. "It's a school night, Caid. We'll go for hamburgers and watch a movie on Friday."

"Yeah!" Caid jumped to the floor. "Will you read me a story, Dad?"

Linc glanced at Selena, unsure about what to do next.

"Go ahead, Linc. Read Caid his story. I can let myself out."

Staring at her, he still wasn't sure what to do. He wanted to tuck his son into bed, read him a story, and lay with him until he fell asleep. He also wanted time with Selena.

"Goodnight, Selena." Caid waved his hand in the air as he dashed down the hall, oblivious to the tug-of-war his dad faced.

"Goodnight, Caid. I'm glad I got to meet you." She clasped her hands together, glancing around, feeling like a third wheel, knowing she needed to leave. Spying her purse on a nearby counter, she flashed Linc a cautious smile. "If you have time, perhaps we can talk tomorrow."

He stepped forward, wrapping his hands around her arms. "You aren't slipping away while I put Caid to bed. You're staying here so we can talk once he's asleep. Or a better idea is for you to join me in his bedroom while I read him a story." All the time he spoke, his hands glided up and down her arms, sparking the desire always hovering between them.

Stepping away, her smiled faltered. "As much as I'd like to stay, I think it's best I leave. You need time with Caid, and I have work in the morning. A woman's got to get her rest, you know." Her attempt at humor fell flat.

"You're not running, are you?"

"I don't know what you mean." Well, she kind of did. Selena had fallen hard for this man, knowing she could do the same for his son. If it didn't work out, the pain would double. She needed time to think and determine if, after such a short period of time, she was willing to put it all on the line for this relationship.

"I think you do. You're trying to decide if it's worth it. One week, you're in a relatively carefree relationship without strings. The next, you're looking at sharing time with me and a young boy. I'm certain you feel it isn't what you signed up for," Linc ground out. She wondered if he referred to her or him. "It would surprise me if you didn't consider backing away." The accusation in his voice surprised her.

She leveled her gaze at him, feeling defensive and confused. "I'm not backing away, and I don't regret the change in your life. We're all handed surprises, which we deal with as best we can."

Crossing his arms, he leaned against a counter, trying to understand why her choosing to take off tonight irritated him. They'd made no commitments, never talked of love or a future, so his reaction made little sense. As much as he wanted to continue giving a relationship with Selena a chance, having Caid in his life had changed everything, including his priorities. Perhaps Selena was right to back off and give them time to adjust to the changes. No matter the physical pleasure they enjoyed with each other, the look on her face warned him that his decision to track her down this morning may have been premature.

"Unlike when we met, Caid is now my first priority. Every decision I make must include how my actions impact him. *Any* relationship I pursue now becomes more complicated."

His words did more than strike a nerve. They seemed to be a warning. At the very least, his last comment indicated Linc didn't share the same feelings she had for him.

"I'd never ask you to decide between Caid and me, if that's what you're implying. That would be insane, selfish, and quite unreasonable." Her voice faltered as the notion he might not want her in his life began to take root.

Picking up her jacket, she speared her arms through the sleeves, securing the buttons, then crossed her arms, fighting for calm. "I do believe it is best for you to take time with Caid, decide what you want or if you even have time for a relationship. As you so plainly stated, *if* you decide to pursue a relationship with anybody, you'll need to consider all the consequences."

Linc cringed, hearing his words slung back at him, seeing the stricken look on her face. "Selena, I didn't mean…"

She waited for him to finish, but his voice trailed off, as if he didn't know what else to say. "You have a lot to consider. Regardless of what transpired between us today, you may decide I'm not what you need." She stopped, taking a moment to control her wavering voice and the ache in her heart. "If having me in your life is what you really want, you know where to find me. I'm only half a lake away."

Sliding her purse over her shoulder, she walked through the foyer, glancing down the hall toward Caid's bedroom—the one right next to Linc's. Her mind reeled at what had transpired the last few minutes. The idea they might not reconcile because of the changes in his life slammed into her.

Closing the door, she forced herself not to run to her car. She'd leave, but with as much dignity as possible. She'd climbed from her bed this morning with the knowledge she'd lost Linc, but his appearance had given her hope it might all work out. Driving home, the same bleak feeling of loss overwhelmed her. Swiping dampness from her cheeks, she gripped the steering wheel, reflecting on their conversation.

Within the span of minutes, she'd gone from the fantasy of pretending to be a part of Linc's life to the reality of being an outsider. She took a deep breath, trying to calm the trembles seeming to overwhelm her. Being on the outside had been the definition of her life.

Quiet and serious, she'd always spent most of her time alone, trying to summon enough courage to face each day the way her sisters did. Even Danielle and Lillian had more confidence than she did. If not for her sisters' support, she'd have spent high school, college, and the years since graduation with little social interaction. The Kerrigan family had always been her safe haven, the only people she could truly count on.

Blinking away the last of her tears, she pulled into her driveway. Turning off the engine, she stayed seated, too overwhelmed to move. She didn't want to enter her house alone or sleep in the same bed she'd shared with Linc hours before.

Making a quick decision, Selena returned to the lake road, driving past the turn to Linc's house, past the town of Pine Cove, then taking the fork in the road toward the main highway and the town of Cedar Springs. Linc had taken her to the quaint mountain settlement not long after they'd returned from their weekend in Spokane. Their first date.

Thirty minutes later, she pulled into a small motel nestled in the trees. Having nothing with her except the clothes she wore, some cash, and a couple credit cards, she finished registering and walked into a charming and clean room. Tossing her purse on the bed, she made a promise to herself to think through what was best for her and not let her life hinge on what Linc did or didn't want. He had legitimate doubts, needed time to settle into his new life with Caid. Her involvement didn't seem to be helping.

Their brief interlude had been wonderful, exhilarating—everything she'd hope to experience and never believed she would. Now she had to face reality. A life with Linc might not be in her future. Pulling out her phone, she sent texts to Julia and Caly, telling them of her decision to take a few days off and not to worry. That simple act helped clear her head. Curling into a ball on the bed, she closed her eyes, determined to make a change. Tomorrow, she'd push Linc from her mind. Sighing, a grim chuckle escaped when she realized ridding him from her heart could take much longer.

Chapter Fourteen

"What do you mean you don't know where she is?" Linc's voice rose a notch. He'd waited until the following day to find Selena and apologize for being such an idiot. Calling wouldn't achieve what he needed. Talking face-to-face so he could see her eyes and reach out to hold her was what he wanted.

He'd had another sleepless night, and it was all his doing. Worse, he couldn't figure out how such an enjoyable evening had turned into a disaster within minutes.

"All Caly and I know is she sent us a text last night saying she wanted to take a few days off and telling us not to worry. She's a grown woman, Linc, and can do what she wants, even if we don't like it." Julia stared at him across the desk, seeing the dark circles under his eyes and lines of worry in his expression. "We assumed she'd still be at her house, but you said her car is gone."

"No sign of it. That's why I came here, hoping I could catch her."

Julia's eyes brightened as she laughed. "I don't believe you have to worry. I'm pretty sure you caught her weeks ago."

"Not after last night." Linc didn't try to hide his frustration as he pushed a hand through his hair.

She leaned forward, her arms resting on the desk, her expression serious. "Tell me what happened."

A few minutes later, Julia sat back, absorbing what Linc shared.

"The whole thing is my fault." Standing, he paced across the room to a bookcase filled with books and family pictures. He picked up one showing the five Kerrigan sisters standing together.

"That was taken at my wedding."

The dull ache in his chest pounded in a painful rhythm as he stared at a smiling Selena, her arms around her two youngest sisters.

"I've never met Danielle and Lillian, although she's mentioned them several times." He set the picture back on the shelf, glanced at a few more, then turned back toward Julia.

"They're still in college. Even though Peregrine Bay isn't far away, they seldom come home, except for holidays and summer break." Julia walked up to him. "Of all of us, Selena is the one who tends to fold into herself when something bothers her. I'm guessing she needs a little time to think through what happened last night. How did the two of you leave it?"

Rubbing a finger across his brow, he recalled her last words. "She said if I wanted her in my life, I'd know where to find her." His pained chuckle told Julia a great deal about how he felt. "I won't push her. When she surfaces, I'd appreciate it if you'd let her know I tried to find her."

"I will. And don't worry. I'm sure this will all work out." Julia knew her words weren't what Linc wanted to hear. He had the look of a man on the brink of making major life decisions. A man who needed a friend, possibly a lover he could count on, yet didn't know quite how to go about it. In the span of a week, the successful, carefree bachelor, who could have a date at the snap of his fingers, had become a father and realized how much he cared for one particular woman. Julia would laugh if it weren't for the desolate look on Linc's face as he closed the door behind him.

Picking up her phone, Julia sent a brief text to Selena. What happened next was up to her sister.

******

Turning onto her back, Selena stretched her arms above her head, opening her eyes. Bolting up, she looked at one unfamiliar wall after another. The disorientation lasted a few moments as her gaze darted from the bed to the dresser. When she spotted her purse, phone, watch, and car keys, emptiness filled her as she remembered the night before, the long drive, and the brief text to her sisters.

Glancing at the clock next to the bed, she exhaled. Almost noon. Her stomach growled, underscoring the fact she hadn't eaten in over sixteen hours, yet all she craved was coffee. And Linc.

Selena rolled out of bed, picked up her phone, and scrolled through the messages. Nothing from Linc, which didn't surprise her, but hurt nevertheless. She read a text from Julia and one from Caly before feeling the phone vibrate, indicating another text had been delivered. Reading the second message from Julia, her lips curved into a tight smile, not sure what to make of Linc trying to find her.

Resisting the urge to call either Linc or Julia, she showered, dressed, and locked the door behind her as she went in search of food. Functioning on an empty stomach had never been productive.

Cedar Springs was comprised of a few square blocks, making it considerably smaller than Peregrine Bay. A major stop for travelers moving between the United States and Canada in the 1800s, it had fallen onto hard times when highways and freeways bypassed it in the twentieth century. The local economy continued to hold its own as either a stopover for those seeking a quaint getaway or a weekend retreat for residents of Spokane.

Finding a cozy restaurant serving breakfast all day, Selena settled into a booth.

"Good afternoon, honey. What can I get you?" A rotund woman with graying brown hair smiled down at her, giving a quick wave to someone walking through the door.

Selena read the name tag. "Coffee with sugar and cream, Agnes. Also, a three egg omelet with ham, onions, mushrooms, and cheese."

The woman raised her brow. "Our omelets are made with jumbo eggs."

"Wonderful." Selena smiled up at her.

"They're about this big." She gestured with her hands so Selena could visualize the size. "I get truckers in here who can't finish one."

"Sounds perfect. Plus an order of biscuits and gravy, please."

Jotting it down, the waitress shook her head. "I'll get your coffee."

The weather had switched from warm and inviting the day before to cold and windy. The lightweight pants and blouse Selena wore weren't warm enough to keep away the shivers.

"Here you go. Cream and sugar are right there." She nodded to a basket holding condiments. "Your food will be out in a few more minutes."

"Thank you. Would you be able to guide me to a store where I can buy some warmer clothes?"

"Well now, Bernadette's is just around the corner. Not fancy, but the prices are good. 'Course, I have to tell you about it because she's my cousin." Agnes winked. "There's also the western shop another block down. It's real popular with the weekend crowd from the city." Bending to look at the flats Selena wore, she laughed. "You may want to buy some warmer shoes, too. You'll find what you want at either of those stores."

"Are you related to the owners of the western shop, too?" Selena's eyes twinkled when Agnes blushed.

"Honey, just about everyone is related to me in this town, some on account of my good-for-nothing ex-husband. But if you mention I sent you, they'll give you a good deal." She smiled as she walked away.

Sighing in satisfaction at her first sip of coffee all day, Selena relaxed in the booth, taking a good look around the café. Old pictures of Cedar Springs covered one wall, and beautiful scenery shots decorated a second. The wall next to where she sat showed state and national dignitaries who'd passed through, as well as well-known local personalities who made their home in Idaho.

Narrowing her gaze, she studied several before she stiffened at one in particular. Wearing the familiar gear of local hunters, Linc, Matt, and Shane stood shoulder to shoulder, cocky grins on their faces.

"Those are the owners of Templar Security & Rescue over near Pine Cove. A darn handsome bunch, don't you think?" Agnes set down a plate overflowing with a huge omelet, then another with two biscuits covered in gravy. "The company donates money to our schools and gun safety program. Real fine people. I'll get you some more coffee." Walking behind the counter, she failed to see the color drain from Selena's face.

She glanced down at the enormous amount of food, stomach roiling. The appetite she'd walked in with had disappeared, replaced by an urgency to grab her purse and leave.

"Something wrong with the food?" Agnes asked as she topped off Selena's cup.

"Um…no. You sure do dish up huge portions." Selena picked up her fork, determined to push the image of Linc from her mind and eat every bite of breakfast. "I may be here awhile."

"You take as long as you want. No one's in much of a hurry in this town."

Groaning at the lumberjack-sized helpings, Selena squared her shoulders. She thought of her vow the night before to focus on her own needs and not think about Linc. Glancing at the photo, she acknowledged it might not be as simple as she first thought. Even with the knowledge he'd stopped by the office asking Julia about her, she still believed letting him settle into his life with Caid, without the added pressure of a relationship, was his best choice. If he still wanted her when his life calmed down, she'd make a decision then. Right now, her goals were simple. Finish the two plates of food, then find some warmer clothes.

******

"Where are we going?" Caid sat in the passenger seat of the long bed truck, a ball cap on his head, action figures in both hands. He couldn't see much more than the tops of the trees out of the front window, which didn't bother him at all.

Linc glanced at him and back to the road, unable to contain a smile. School had let out early, and even though Nina had been prepared to pick Caid up, he wanted to be there himself.

"A group of friends are meeting at a park. I thought you'd enjoy it."

Caid's gaze shot to Linc, the animated figures coming to a stop in his hands. "Will there be other kids?"

"Yeah, buddy. I'm pretty sure there will be." When he wasn't trying to find Selena, he'd spent most of the day calling around to locate friends who'd be willing to come by the park. It wasn't a long list when he didn't include Matt, Shane, or Selena.

Selena. He still hadn't heard from her. He hated the way she'd left the house the night before, knowing she felt angry, hurt, and confused. Linc felt the same. Too much had happened between them in too short a time. Then Caid had appeared, creating an entirely new dynamic. Accepting his son had become his first priority, Linc agreed with Selena that the two needed time together to bond, get to know each other. He just hadn't thought it would come at the exclusion of her from his life. The easy solution would be to let her go, build a life with his son, continue to grow TSR, and find companionship with an occasional woman. One who'd want little from him, other than the occasional date and emotionless sex.

Unfortunately, Linc no longer wanted one-night stands or sex based on some tacit agreement not to become involved. He wanted a warm, soft body nestled next to his each night, glances shared by two people who knew each other so well they didn't need words, and a partner who'd have his back like he'd have hers.

One image flashed across his mind. Selena. He never should've let her leave until they'd talked it out, or at least agreed about how they would continue seeing each other while he got to know Caid. Even if he wasn't ready to make a permanent commitment, Linc knew he wasn't ready to lose her from his life either.

"Here we are." He parked the truck near a group of men and women, kids of various ages playing around them.

Within minutes, Caid became absorbed into the crowd of rowdy children. Watching him take off after a ball, Linc joined the adults.

"So that's your son."

Linc glanced to his side to see a woman he'd dated a few times standing next to him. A divorcée with a young daughter, he'd decided to back off, not wanting Heather to assume too much by his attention. He'd been focused on TSR, having no interest in anything serious. She'd taken it well, although he knew the decision disappointed her.

Today, she'd pulled her auburn hair into a loose ponytail and wore little makeup, making Heather appear closer to twenty than the twenty-eight he knew to be her age.

"It is. His name is Caiden, but he prefers Caid."

"And you didn't know he existed until last week?" Heather walked closer to where the children played, getting a better look at Linc's son.

"Not a clue. He lived with his mother's family after she died. And before you ask, yes, I was married before. It was brief and I hadn't had any contact with her since."

"Well, she left you a beautiful son, Linc. You should be very happy about it. I don't know what I'd do without Sadie."

They continued with casual conversation, joining the other parents as the kids played. When the sun set, they gathered by their cars, Heather coming up to him with Sadie by her side.

"If you ever want to talk about parenting, or drop Caid off to play with Sadie, let me know." She saw the wary look on Linc's face and laughed. "No strings. I'm dating a man from Peregrine Bay, a firefighter. This is just an offer from one parent to another."

Linc's face softened. "I'd appreciate any tips you can offer, as long as your boyfriend doesn't object."

"Not an issue. He trusts me completely." Heather watched as Caid held out an action figure to Sadie. She took it, twirling it like a miniature baton.

"How about tomorrow? It's an early school day. We'll drive someplace and let the kids play while you school me on the specifics of parenthood."

"Perfect." Heather slipped her hand into Sadie's, walking toward her car. "We can meet at the school and go from there. I'll bring the lunches."

"We'll see you tomorrow."

******

A loud horn woke Selena from a deep, dreamless sleep. Realizing it wasn't an alarm, she sat up, thankful for the warmth of the flannel drawstring pants and long-sleeved cotton t-shirt she'd found at Bernadette's. The clock flashed nine o'clock. If she weren't in Cedar Springs, she'd already be in her office, fielding emails and phone calls.

Pulling on the running clothes she'd purchased, Selena stretched her arms above her head, bending toward her toes, then rising, ready to head outside. Slipping into a hoodie, she closed the door behind her, noticing the low cloud cover and slight drizzle. Taking off along the highway, she thought of

Linc, wondering if he were at his office or still taking time at home with Caid. As the pain began to rise, she picked up the pace, pounding the hurt away with each stride.

An hour later, breathing heavily but feeling a bit better, she returned to her room. Several minutes under the hot shower also helped. Pulling on new jeans and a light blue turtleneck sweater, she checked her phone for emails and texts. She didn't feel quite as disappointed as yesterday when she saw nothing from Linc. Perhaps the time apart had been a good decision after all.

Snatching her purse off the dresser, she left for the café.

"Good morning, Agnes."

"Ah, you returned. Coffee and omelet?" Agnes walked over to the booth Selena chose, setting down a cup and filling it.

"Not this morning. I have to concede you were right about the omelets," she laughed. "I think oatmeal with fruit would be perfect."

Agnes stopped by a few more times, filling her cup, making sure everything was fine, then set down the check.

"What are your plans today?" Agnes asked as she took Selena's credit card.

"I ran past a beautiful park about two miles north of here during my run this morning. I think I'll drive back, take pictures, and explore the area."

"Wear sturdy shoes. There are some winding trails to the top. Take any one of them for about half an hour. You won't be disappointed."

******

"Are we almost there, Dad?"

Linc looked at the two children in his rearview mirror. They'd been on the road twenty minutes.

"Not long, Caid."

Linc and Heather shared a look, trying to hide their amusement. Sadie had asked the same question not ten minutes before, getting the same answer.

"How long does this go on?" Linc asked.

"How long before you stopped asking the same thing when you went on car trips with your parents? I know I must've been at least thirteen." Heather laughed at the look of horror on Linc's face.

"You mean I have another seven years of this?"

"At least." She glanced out the window. "Look. There's a park next to the creek." The clouds had blown away, replaced by a clear blue sky.

Turning off the road, Linc found a parking spot. "All right, kids. We're here."

A chorus of squeals signaled their excitement as they jumped out of the truck and ran toward the water.

"You grab the blanket and follow them. I'll bring the food and drinks." Linc picked up the wicker basket, then walked to where Heather had spread a blanket next to a table under a large spruce tree.

"I think this spot will work out great. We can see the kids and talk without them hearing." Heather pulled a soda out of the cooler and took a seat at the table, popping the top and taking a long swallow. "I allow myself one soda a day around noon. It seems to fortify me for the rest of the day."

"Guess that leaves a lunchtime whiskey out." Linc picked up his own soda, sitting next to Heather. "Okay, I'm ready for your sage advice. I've got a lot to learn in a short period of time."

"You know, this is a lifelong educational experience. No parent ever learns all there is in one sitting. In fact, I don't believe it's ever possible to learn enough." She placed a hand on his arm. "Relax, Linc. You'll make a great parent."

He watched Caid and Sadie splash each other with water, then run in circles chasing a butterfly. "Thanks, Heather. It's a little more overwhelming than I first thought, but Caid means everything to me. I'm determined to make it work."

She leaned over, placing a congenial arm around his shoulders, kissing his cheek. "You're going to be wonderful."

******

Taking the trail back toward the creek, Selena took her time, snapping pictures at will. She'd always loved photography, the challenge of getting the right angle, the right light. A few of her pictures were framed, buried in a box in her garage. Someday, when she got the nerve, Selena had every intention of taking them out and filling a wall with them. Until then, she'd keep snapping away, hoping to get the perfect shot.

The sound of children's laughter had her taking a right instead of a left at the fork. She followed the path, stopping when she saw a girl and boy giggling, chasing each other in a game of tag.

Bringing her phone up, she took several shots, then moved closer until she stood on the other side of the creek. Snapping a couple more, she stepped on a series of rocks traversing the water, creating a crossing.

Selena watched a few more minutes before turning toward an open area with picnic tables.

Walking around a stand of large trees, she came to an abrupt stop a few feet away from a couple at a nearby table, the woman's arm around the man's shoulders.

Her breath hitched when the man turned to her, his eyes widening.

"Selena." Linc stood. "Can you watch Caid for me?"

"Of course. Go. The kids will be fine," Heather answered, watching as he took long, determined strides toward the woman.

Selena hadn't expected to run into him already spending time with someone else a few days after their argument. And it wasn't the nanny this time.

Turning, she started walking away, trying to pretend what she'd seen hadn't been real.

"What are you doing here?" Linc grabbed her arm, spinning her around. "I went by your house, your office, but no one knew where you were."

Shrugging out of his hold, Selena glanced over his shoulder. "I'm taking some time away. It appears you're doing the same."

Looking behind him, Linc sighed. Twice now she'd thought he'd been with someone else. This had to stop.

"This is not what you think. Heather and I are friends. She has a girl the same age as Caid. She offered to give me tips on parenting, which I sorely need."

"Right. Tips." She cringed at the way her voice dripped with sarcasm. Shaking her head, she caught her lower lip between her teeth and sighed. "That was uncalled for. You can see anyone you want."

Placing his hands on her shoulders, he studied her face. "Really? Then I want to see *you*. Tonight. Just you and me for dinner away from the house. Nina can watch Caid."

It felt as if the anger, along with her breath, had been forced out of her. Blinking a few times, she tried to back away, but his grip held steady.

"I don't know what happened between us the other night and I don't care. All I know is I want to continue seeing you, figure out if we have any kind of future. I also know I have no desire to see anyone else." He leaned in, brushing his lips across hers. "What do you say?"

Lips curving into a tentative smile, she nodded. "I already paid for another night at the motel."

"I'll take care of it."

"I need to get my things."

"We'll follow you to the motel, then you can follow us back to Peregrine Bay. I have to drop Heather off at the school for her car, then take Caid home. I'll pick you up at seven." He kissed her again, then once more before letting his hands drop to his sides. "All right?"

"Yes. I think I'd like that."

Chapter Fifteen

"I have the first attack on TSR set up for later tonight, C. It should do what your stepdaddy wants." Rave's voice held a strange edge mingled with excitement. "If all goes right, TSR won't be able to neutralize it for a few hours."

C gripped the phone tighter, the news bittersweet. "It won't destroy their systems, right?"

"Nah. Just mess with them long enough for their clients to know their services were compromised. It may not be enough to change their reputation, but I'll set something up for tomorrow, then again the following day. Three incidences in less than thirty-six hours will shake client confidence."

"Are you certain nothing can be traced back to either of us?"

"Positive, C. No matter what TSR's tech guru tries, our identities are off the grid. Guaranteed." Rave's deep breathing for several moments was all that could be heard over the phone. "I'll let you know when the first one hits. If you know how to contact their clients, I'd suggest anonymous phone calls to notify them of possible threats. Give them a heads-up their data is at risk. Be sure to use a burner phone. You don't want to leave a trail."

"Got it, Rave." It was time to make another phone call.

"I'll be in touch." Rave hung up, a smug smile crossing his face. C had been a good friend when everyone else had turned their back on him. Whatever his friend asked, Rave would do his best to make it happen. He couldn't wait to hear the shock in C's voice when the surprise he'd set up was eventually discovered. All the time and effort he'd put into this would be worth it. Plus, his friend would be that much closer to having a normal life.

******

"You have word for me?" Even at this hour of the night, Ephraim sounded wide awake.

"First phase goes off tonight. But I have terms."

"Terms?" Ephraim laughed. "I'm calling the shots, not you."

"Maybe in the past, but no longer. I want mother taken care of without your continued blackmail. Obtaining the contract for the arts center will set Simondson Security up as a solid player in Idaho, which is what you want. With what I have planned, you'll be able to knock a major blow to TSR on this bid and going forward. Now, here's the deal. I want two hundred thousand transferred into a bank account within the hour. I'll give you the information. Once it's in my account, I trigger the action to start. No money, no results."

Silence stretched for long minutes before Ephraim's angry voice seemed to jump through the phone. "You listen to me—"

"No, you listen. This ends tonight with me having the money to take care of mother. You get what you want and I get what she's owed. You can wash your hands of her, which is what you've wanted for a long time. Take it or leave it."

"You're certain what you have planned will work?"

"Without a doubt." Rave's confidence was catching. The man knew his stuff.

"If I find you're screwing with me, no amount of money will protect you."

"Then we have a deal?"

"Yes, but heed my warning. This better work." Ephraim's irate voice emphasized his words.

"It will. Here is the transfer information you need."

******

"You'll be good for Nina, right, Caid?" Linc knelt down next to his son, who was focused on the action figures spread out in front of him.

"Uh-huh." His head bobbed, but he didn't look at his father.

"Do I get a hug?"

Caid stood, wrapped his arms around Linc, then dropped back down on the floor without a word.

Linc glanced up at Nina, who shrugged.

"We'll be fine, Mr. Caldwell. Go on and have a good time."

"I don't know how late I'll be." Linc stood, but didn't turn to leave.

"That's why you provide a bedroom for me." Nina moved closer to him, lowering her voice. "He'll be fine. I suggest you take off while he's concentrating on his toys."

"Call me if you need anything. Even if he just wants to talk to me." He still didn't take his gaze off Caid, waiting to see if his son glanced up at him.

"I will."

Nodding, Linc walked through the house and into the garage, sliding into his sleek black sports car. He sat a few minutes before turning the engine over and driving through the gates on his way to Selena's, feeling his world tilt as he turned onto the highway.

Less than two months ago, he'd been in control of every aspect of his life. Not now. Linc always prided himself on setting goals, attaining them, then raising the bar. He'd thought the brief marriage to Valerie had been a colossal mistake until he learned the union had produced a son. Although not a bullet point on his list of goals, none of his other accomplishments compared to Caid. Graduating from the Naval Academy, becoming a SEAL, or the phenomenal success of TSR didn't come close to the joy he experienced with his son.

His growing feelings for Selena hadn't been planned either. What started as one evening together in Spokane shifted into them spending almost every night in either her bed or his. He still couldn't figure it out. Their relationship had developed into a desire and passion he'd never experienced in his past relationships. Not even with Valerie.

Linc chuckled, remembering what his mother had told him years before about accepting real love when it smacked him in the backside. Perhaps this was the real deal, unexpected and slamming into him like a Texas tornado.

Lacking any other explanation, he pulled into Selena's driveway, determined to make tonight a new start for them both.

******

"I haven't been here in a long time." As Linc pulled out her chair, Selena glanced around the elegant restaurant inside the oldest hotel in Peregrine Bay. Her stepmother, Joannie, called it "elegantly understated." Antique furniture of cherry wood, walnut, rosewood, and mahogany graced the dining room. The chairs were covered in rich brocade. Surprisingly, instead of the walls being covered in wallpaper, they'd been painted a soft cream shade and were adorned with beautiful landscapes of the surrounding mountains and lakes. A large painting of Lake Bountiful hung above the massive fireplace, a perfect background for their table.

"I've never been here at all. Heather mentioned it when I told her about our dinner plans."

Selena waited until Linc ordered wine. "Tell me about Heather."

"Not much to tell. She went through a divorce a few years ago, we went on a couple dates, nothing serious, and now she's seeing a firefighter in town." He took a sip of wine, then nodded to their waiter.

"You know, my cousin, Devlin, is part of the Lake Bountiful Hotshots. I wonder if he knows Heather."

He thought back, not recalling Selena ever mentioning her cousin. "Have I met Devlin?"

"Not through me, but he was at the party at your house when you and I met. I believe a female friend invited him. Truthfully, I never know with Dev. Like you, he's always got someone different on his arm." She glanced over the rim of her wine glass, knowing she'd baited him.

Linc's expression stilled at the barb. "That's not me anymore, Selena. The only woman I want on my arm is you."

She had no comeback for that, choosing to hide the color warming her face behind the menu.

He tilted his head toward hers. "No response?"

Letting the menu dip lower, enough to see the serious expression on his face, she reconsidered a sharp retort. Lowering her hands, she leaned toward him, brushing her lips against his. "I like the idea of being the only woman on your arm."

"Good. At least we're together on that point."

"Selena?" They broke apart, each glancing at the man standing next to their table. "I thought that was you."

She blinked a couple times, not expecting to see Chad again so soon after running into him at the event in Spokane.

"Good evening, Chad."

"It's good to see you again." He held out his hand, flashing what she used to consider a megawatt smile.

She grasped his hand, releasing it in a quick motion.

Turning, he extended his hand to Linc, who now stood beside him.

"Do you have business in Peregrine Bay?" She kept her expression neutral, praying his presence in town was brief.

"Yes, but I'm not certain for how long. As I mentioned in Spokane, my stepfather asked me to represent his firm to prospects throughout Idaho. This is my base of operations for now."

"So what is it you do, Chad?" Linc's gaze bored into his.

"My company provides security equipment and services. Simondson Security. Perhaps you've heard of it." As if on cue, the cocky grin Selena remembered appeared on Chad's face.

"Yes, I'm familiar with them." *Too familiar*, Linc thought, believing their encounter in the restaurant hadn't been by accident. "Well, it was a pleasure seeing you again. I hope you don't mind, but tonight is rather special for Selena and me." Linc inclined his head toward the table as the waiter set their plates down.

"No problem. Selena, perhaps we can meet for coffee or lunch sometime soon." Reaching in a pocket, he handed her his card. "Give me a call when you have a chance. Linc, nice to see you again." Without another word, Chad left them alone, returning to a table across the room.

Selena watched him leave, sucking in a quick breath when she recognized his tablemate, Councilman Tom Harten.

******

Linc kept a close watch on Selena during their drive back to her place and while she made coffee, her fingers shaking when she handed him a cup.

"Are you going to tell me about Chad? Or do I have to guess?" He kept his voice soft, hoping she'd confide in him. After Chad walked away from their table, she'd closed up, talking little during the rest of their dinner. He wanted to know why.

Taking a seat next to him on the sofa, she waved a hand in the air, hoping a condensed version would satisfy him. "Chad's just a guy I met in college. I may have mentioned about going to a party after graduation." Linc nodded. "Well, he's the one who invited me, but not as a date. He disappeared not long after I arrived. I drove home a couple hours later. That's it." Not a complete account, but close enough.

"And?"

"And what? That's all. I never saw him again after that night."

Setting his cup down, he grabbed her around the waist and lifted her onto his lap. "Sweetheart, we've been together long enough for you to be honest with me. I'm not buying your version. Why don't you tell me the unabridged story? All of it."

******

"Son of a bitch," Linc muttered, holding her close, his body vibrating as Selena finished her story. Considering how much she resisted telling him, her voice had remained strong, without the emotion he expected.

"The strange part is, I don't think any of my sisters would've been upset about stumbling on Chad the way I did. Why does it still send chills through me after all this time?"

Stroking a hand down Selena's hair, he kissed her forehead. "We're all unique and react to situations differently. Even years later, some things just stick with us."

"True, but that doesn't account for overreacting to what I saw and carrying it with me after all these years."

"Walking in on something like that, unprepared and with little experience, would upset most anyone."

She glanced up at him. "Not you."

He chuckled. "No, not me. Selena, you need to understand the men, and some of the women, I've been around most of my life would consider what you saw pretty tame. You aren't like me or them. How many porn flicks have you ever seen?"

She sat up, pushing away from him. "None."

"Strip clubs?"

"Um, none."

"Not even Chippendales?"

Pushing herself off his lap, she stood, pacing a few feet away. "You make me sound pathetic."

"Not being into those activities doesn't make you pathetic at all. You have a strong sense of who you are and won't allow yourself to be pressured into doing something outside your comfort zone. There's nothing wrong with that. In fact, it's to be admired." He walked up to her, placing his hands on her shoulders. "I admire it." Bending down, he kissed the sensitive area below her ear.

"Yeah?" She sucked in a breath, tilting her head to give him better access.

"Oh, yeah." He trailed kisses along her jaw and down to the hollow at the base of her neck. "There is so much about you I admire, Selena." His deep, husky voice sent chills through her a moment before he claimed her mouth with his.

She moaned as his hands gripped her hips, drawing her close, the heat scorching through the fabric of her dress, burning her skin. His mouth slanted against hers, his tongue urgent and searching as it slipped between her parted lips. She squirmed against him, feeling the familiar tightness deep in her stomach as her knees began to buckle, a soft moan spilling from her lips.

Wrapping her hands behind his neck, she drew him close, sliding her fingers through his hair. Linc's deep groan sent shivers through her body, fire streaming through every limb.

Drawing her hands to his shirt, she released the buttons, splaying fingers across the hard, warm surface of his chest. Her body hummed with desire as another groan escaped his lips.

Feeling Linc lift her against his chest, Selena wrapped her legs around him, cradling his face as she kissed his lips.

Pulling away, he took a long, deep breath, his gaze raking over her face. "You are so beautiful, Selena. So damn beautiful." He dragged in a ragged breath, taking long strides into her bedroom, lowering her, then lying down beside her.

"You are the woman I want. Don't ever doubt it." Feathering kisses along her shoulder to her neck, his lips burned a path to her mouth, feeling her shiver against him.

"Linc, I can't wait any longer. Please." It came out as a soft plea, her hands spearing into his hair.

"Sweetheart, neither can I."

Chapter Sixteen

Linc's fingers twirled a strand of Selena's hair as she sprawled on top of him. He knew the sun would peek through the windows in a couple hours and he had to head home, back to Caid and his responsibilities.

The thought of leaving her chilled him as much as not being home when his son ran into his room, his hands loaded with action figures, and climbed onto the bed. A brief ritual, but one Linc looked forward to each morning.

Letting out a groan, he released the strand of hair, then carefully lifted Selena's arm off his chest before sliding out from under her. Regret at losing her warmth, her touch, hit him with such force, he almost wished he hadn't moved. But his new life called like a siren, signaling his need to leave.

"Where are you going?" Selena's sleepy voice mumbled as she rolled to her back and sat up, drawing the covers up under her chin.

"I believe it's a little late for you to turn modest around me." He chuckled, then leaned down, giving her a warm kiss. Breaking it before he took her in his arms, he straightened. "Caid will be awake in a couple hours."

"Ah…" She rubbed her eyes, then tossed the covers aside, picking up a V-neck tee from the day before. "I'll make coffee."

He stopped buttoning his shirt, a sensation he couldn't quite place settling in his chest. "You don't have to do that."

"But I want to." Her sleepy smile did nothing to cool the desire he felt for this woman. In that moment, Linc knew he had to find a way to keep her in his life. He started to open his mouth when the sounds of a country song indicated an incoming call. Tearing his gaze away from Selena, he grabbed his phone.

"Caldwell," he answered when he saw Matt's face pop up on the screen.

"We have a situation. It's not good." Matt used the code they'd set up for matters of extreme urgency, requiring all the key people to be present. "Shane and I are already here."

"I'll be there in twenty minutes. Call Tina."

"Will do."

Linc slid the phone in his pocket and walked around the bed, seeing the concern on Selena's face. "I'll need to take a raincheck on the coffee."

"It's not Caid, is it?"

Shaking his head, he stroked a finger down her face, then cupped her cheek, leaning in for a kiss which should have lasted much longer.

"Something at work. I'll need to call Nina and have her stay longer with Caid."

"I'll go. She needs a break and I'd like to help." Her gaze shot to his, realizing she may have overstepped whatever boundaries Linc had set around his son.

"You wouldn't mind?"

Grabbing a pair of jeans, she slipped her legs in, pulling up the zipper. "I'd love to spend time with him, as long as you're okay with the idea of your girlfriend helping out."

Reaching out, Linc snaked an arm around her waist, pulling her close. "I definitely like the idea of my girlfriend hanging out with my son." He crushed his mouth to hers, sweeping his tongue inside before lessening the pressure, brushing his lips across hers once more, then stepped back.

"Of course, it will cost you." Glazed eyes sparkled, her mouth tilting into a smug grin.

"Ah, sweetheart. Those are words I live for."

******

"Tell me what you know." Linc shrugged out of his jacket, tossing it on a table, and took a seat between Shane and Matt.

"A sophisticated hit on our system about an hour before Matt called. See this?" Shane pointed to his screen. "This isn't some random attack by an amateur. It's serious shit, Linc."

"Phreaker's still working on it. He caught it before any real damage was done." Matt took a long swallow from a can of Dr. Pepper, his normal drink of choice when working.

"Clients?" Linc glanced at Tina before leaning forward, deciphering what he saw on Shane's screen.

"Nothing from any of them yet, sir."

"Tina, you're killing me. Call me Linc or Lincoln, but not sir. Am I clear?"

"Sorry. It's a habit I'll work on breaking."

"Phreaker doesn't think the breach caused damage to client data or access to their files." Shane rubbed his eyes.

185

He'd been working late, pushing aside the latest argument with his girlfriend, when Phreaker called. "When he finishes his checks, we'll know more."

As Matt and Shane continued their work and Tina monitored client communication, Linc left to find a cup of coffee. Activity in the customer contact room didn't reflect anything unusual, signaling Phreaker had caught the attempted breach early and neutralized it.

Sipping his coffee, he thought of the upsurge in attacks. The increase in incidences over the last few weeks wasn't normal or acceptable. Linc didn't believe these were random attempts to try and hack into any unsecured system, but were targeted directly at TSR and their clients. In his mind, the reason for the increase, as well as the possible person or persons behind them, seemed clear.

Simondson Security hadn't been happy when they weren't selected for a prominent job in Boise. Everyone, including Linc, had been surprised when the award went to TSR. He knew they deserved the award, assuming they were the lowest bidder as budget had been a prime factor in the selection. Until that point, the two companies had been friendly competitors, crossing paths on occasion with Simondson always filling the role of big dog, the vendor most everyone wanted to use. Not any longer. More than six years of hard work, countless sleepless nights, excessive networking, and access to cutting edge technology had paid off. TSR now stood at the top of the hill, and Ephraim Simondson wasn't a gracious loser.

"Linc?" Tina poked her head into the lounge as he poured another cup of coffee. "Matt and Shane want to talk with you."

Nodding, he followed her through the hallway to room 77C, wondering what he'd missed on her résumé, glad Matt had pushed to hire her. He remembered not thinking she had the background or level of experience TSR needed. Her competence during the kidnapping episode, ability to change directions on short notice, and willingness to accept any challenge had changed Linc's mind.

"What have you heard from Phreaker?" Linc set his cup down, leaning over Shane's shoulder.

"We're clear. He's working on tracking down the source." Shane stood, stretching his arms above his head, letting out a groan. "Why don't you go back to your kid, Linc? Matt and I will keep watch, and Tina can handle any client communication, although they don't seem to be aware of what happened."

"I don't like leaving when you two have been up most of the night."

Matt clasped a hand on Linc's shoulder. "I hate to break this to you, bro, but by the look of you, I don't think you've had much sleep either. Go on home to your son and your lady. We're good here."

******

"Are you ready?" Selena stood several feet in front of Caid, a ball in her hand.

187

Licking his lips, his face scrunched in concentration, Caid gripped the bat in both hands and nodded.

"Okay. Here it comes." She tossed the ball in a soft arc, holding her breath as he readied the bat and swung. "Oh my." Clapping her hands, her gaze moved between the ball and Caid's surprised expression.

"I hit it!" Caid jumped up and down, still holding the bat as the ball skidded across the lawn toward the lake. His eyes wide, he stared at Selena. "Did you see it?"

"I sure did."

"Can we do it again?" He took his place behind the line of string Selena had placed on the ground, unaware of Linc standing on the patio, his arms crossed, a smile on his face.

"We sure can, but you'll need to go get the ball."

Dropping the bat, Caid took off at a run.

Selena's heart hummed at a fast pace when she noticed Linc stalking toward her, his gaze unwavering and intent, face devoid of expression. Licking her lips, she took a step back, her face heating.

"I didn't know you were back."

Not answering, he stopped so close, his chest brushed against her. Without a word, he wrapped a hand behind her head, drawing her toward him as he lowered his mouth. Raking his hands through her hair, he held her steady, deepening the kiss, forgetting the audience a few feet away.

"Ew, Dad. That's gross," Caid groaned.

Pulling back, Linc glanced down at the disgusted expression on his son's face, then looked back at Selena with a wry grin. "He won't think so in a few years," he whispered, kissing her once more. "That was some hit, Caid."

Caid's face instantly turned into a smile. "You saw it?"

"Not only that, I've been watching for a while." Linc crouched, holding out his hand for the ball. "I guess we need to get a few more of these."

"Like, maybe a hundred, huh, Dad?"

Linc bit back a smile at Caid's pleading words. "Well, at least another ten or twelve. Maybe we can find a store before dinner. That is, if Selena agrees to join us."

"Oh, I don't—" Selena began.

"Please, Selena," Caid begged.

"You *are* the coach and should have final say on his equipment." Linc grinned when her face colored. He loved the way he could make her blush.

"Yeah," Caid agreed, fiercely nodding his head.

She laughed at the sincerity on both their faces. "I'd be honored to join you."

******

"What about this one, Dad?" Caid held up a jersey displaying the Seattle Mariners logo.

"I thought you were a Pirates fan."

"Nooo." He dragged the single word out. "Grandfather likes the Pirates. I like the Mariners."

"You know, Linc, most people around here tend to support the Washington teams." Selena held back her laughter at the disgust on his face.

"Seems I'm going to be outnumbered on this." He wouldn't mention he was more of a football than baseball fan, although he had followed the Yankees when he went to the Naval Academy. "Let's make sure it fits." Slipping the jersey over Caid's head, he stepped back. "What do you think, Selena?"

"I think you have a potential big leaguer living in the house."

"Guess you'll need something to wear when baseball season rolls around," Linc conceded, although he'd never intended to leave the store without it.

Caid pumped his arm up and down. "Yes!"

"Okay, we have a dozen balls, a helmet, new glove, and the jersey. Let's get out of here." Linc pulled out his wallet as he stepped up to the cashier. Handing the lady his card, he winced at the sound of his phone. Glancing at the caller ID, he turned to Selena. "Sorry, I need to take this. Can you sign for me?"

"Sure."

He stepped away from the counter, answering his phone. "What's up, Matt?"

"You aren't going to believe this, but we have another serious attempt to hack the system. Phreaker says whoever it is went about it a little different this time."

"Can he contain it before the clients are alerted?" Linc turned to look over his shoulder, seeing Selena and Caid standing next to a football display.

"The clients are calling us. Apparently, a few have received anonymous calls telling them our system has been breached and their data compromised. It's pure bull, but the clients don't know that."

Linc lowered his voice, cursing under his breath. "Who the hell are they and what's their intention?"

"Don't know the answer to the first question. The second is obvious. Our success has made TSR a target, which is never a good thing. I'd bet my last dollar it's Simondson or one of the other firms we've beat out in the last couple years. Someone is getting tired of our winning percentage. Phreaker is working on tracking the source, but the first priority is thwarting the attack. You're right, though. Our man needs help, and sooner rather than later."

"I need to take Selena and Caid home, then I'll come in." Linc paused at what he'd said about taking them home. The comment seemed so natural and right. He cleared his throat. "I'll contact my guy on the way to the office."

"Does he know Phreaker?"

"No, but he will." Linc hung up, sliding the phone back into his pocket, joining Caid and Selena at the Seattle Seahawks display. "I suppose you're going to root for the Seahawks, too."

Caid shook his head. "Maybe. Selena and I kind of like the Steelers."

Linc slapped a hand to his forehead in mock surprise. "Steelers?"

"What team do you like?" Selena leaned toward him, sliding an arm through his.

"The Packers. I mean, who doesn't like a team owned by the entire town?" Pulling out his keys, he pressed a kiss to Selena's temple. "We need to get going."

Selena cocked her head, narrowing her gaze at him. "Another issue at work?"

"I'm afraid so. I need to call Nina and ask her to come over."

"No, I'll stay with Caid."

"It may be another late night." Linc cringed at the thought of another sleepless night. "You can sleep in my bed." He unlocked the truck and opened the door, watching as Caid jumped into the back seat.

"Is that a good idea with Caid's room so close?"

"That's one of the reasons I want you in there. If he wakes up, my room is the first place he'll go."

"And the other reason?" Selena asked, her brows lifting.

He ran a hand down her hair, cupping her cheek. "I'd think that would be obvious."

Chapter Seventeen

"Identifying the server will take more time, but the threat has been eliminated for now."

"Are you sure, Phreaker? We need to give our clients an update and can't afford a miscommunication at this point." Shane turned up the volume so Linc, Matt, and Tina could hear.

"We're good, man. Whoever it is, they're real talented. But I'm better." Phreaker's confidence never wavered, a trait Linc appreciated and respected.

"How much sleep have you gotten the last few days?" Linc knew the man must be running on a combination of adrenaline and caffeine.

"Hey, dude, I'm good. Not to worry."

"You didn't just call me *dude*, did you?" Linc shook his head. Humor had always been their relief when on missions with their SEAL team.

"Hey, I'm from California. Deal with it. And while you're at it, can you please delete Phreaker from your vocabulary? I seriously hate that moniker. Call me Tomás or Vega or Awesome Tech Genius. Your choice."

They all laughed, including Tina. She'd heard about his hatred of the nickname he'd been given in the Navy.

"No worries, Vega. I think we can learn to accommodate you." Matt looked at the others. Tina nodded, Shane shrugged, and Linc ignored them all, his expression neutral.

"You and I need to speak, Vega. I'll call you back in ten." Linc hung up before turning toward the hall. "I'll be back after the call."

Shane's brows furrowed as he turned toward Matt. "What's that about?"

"I'm guessing Linc got in touch with his other contact. The one he wants to work with Phreak…I mean Vega. I don't believe he thinks Vega is going to take it very well."

"Yeah, I don't imagine he will."

******

"What do you mean *no*?" Linc's voice signaled his irritation. Partly because of lack of sleep, and partly because he wasn't used to his orders being rejected.

"It's English, man. Let me clear it up for you. No, I don't need help. I've got this covered."

Linc pushed a hand through his thick hair. "Look, Tomás, you've got to be more exhausted than any of us, and we're fried. This guy can pick right up with no hand-holding, and he's known to us—another ex-SEAL. Tell me what your issue is?"

"I don't need someone looking over my shoulder all the time, messing up my work, putting TSR at more risk." Vega's voice sounded strained, irritated. "Besides, you know I can go days without sleep, the same as you. We've lived though much worse than this."

"True. The difference is we no longer have to. He's going to be doing other work for TSR, activated to assist you

194

only when threats like the latest ones escalate. We need a backup for you. As good as you are, there will be times we'll need more resources." Linc paused before dropping the last bomb. "Westfall starts tomorrow."

Linc held the phone away from his ear as a string of curses exploded from Vega. Leaning against the edge of his desk, he let him vent, knowing the man would eventually run out of steam.

"Hell, Linc. Why didn't you tell me up front you'd already hired him?"

"For one, if you had valid reasons for not wanting Gray Westfall on your team, I would've honored them."

"I don't have a *team*, Linc," Vega shot back.

"You do now."

******

Linc pushed open his bedroom door, relief flooding him at the sight of Selena sleeping on his side of the bed. Tossing his jacket on a chair and slipping out of his shoes, he stepped around the bed, noticing a small lump, Selena's arm resting over it. Leaning down, he pulled back the covers, not surprised to see a sleeping Caid.

At three in the morning, he was torn between disturbing his peaceful slumber to return him to his own bed, and crashing on the sofa across the room. The overwhelming desire to share his bed with Selena won out.

"Come on, son," he whispered, slipping his arms under Caid. Not waking, his eyes fluttered as Linc walked to his room and set him down in his bed, tucking the covers around him. Straightening, he watched Caid's breath come out in soft puffs. His heart swelled at the knowledge this small boy belonged to him, connected to Linc in a way no other person had ever been. The knot in his chest tightened as he took a silent vow to do all in his power to keep Caid safe.

Leaving the door ajar, he returned to his room, then stripped off his clothes. Slipping into bed, he pulled Selena close, tucking her tight against his chest, repeating the silent vow he'd made to Caid—this time, including the woman who had burrowed her way into his life and heart.

Brushing a kiss across her brow, he closed his eyes, believing sleep would claim him within minutes. Instead, his mind continued to cycle through the events of the last few days. He'd called Gray Westfall to confirm their earlier discussion, bringing him up to date on the latest threats. Regardless of Vega's objections, Westfall was solid and would make an excellent addition to TSR. The corners of Linc's mouth lifted as he recalled the muttered oath Vega had made to his final comment.

"Westfall is now a part of TSR. Deal with it."

Shane, Matt, and he had already agreed Gray would be brought into the inner circle. Along with Vega, five people would now shape the future of TSR, building a legacy which had now become critically important to Linc.

His thoughts turned to the recent series of attacks. They needed to identify the source. If it were anyone other than Ephraim Simondson, he would be surprised. The man had become obsessed with thwarting the attempts by any firm to usurp Simondson's place as a premier security provider in the northwest. The man was in denial. Almost two years ago, TSR had commandeered first place, leaving Ephraim's company a distant second. Few men took defeat in stride, but none were more vocal in their contempt at being displaced than Simondson.

They just needed proof. That was why he needed both Vega and Westfall working on the issue. His gut told him the threat was far from over, and Linc didn't know how many more targeted attacks TSR could explain to their clients.

******

Selena woke to bright light streaming through the blinds, strong arms holding her tight against a wall of solid muscle. She'd dreamed of waking in Linc's arms, each morning signaling a day full of surprises and challenges. Blinking to clear her head, she tried to slide out of his embrace, only to find herself clutched within his bands of steel.

"Where do you think you're going?" Linc's husky voice stilled her movements as his mouth sucked lightly on the sensitive skin of her neck, then trailed kisses along her shoulder. She arched into him, feeling his hands splay across her stomach.

Sighing, she relaxed against him, relishing each kiss, each caress, wishing they didn't have to stop.

"Caid will be coming in soon." Her already sleepy voice became sultry, her need increasing with each touch. Turning to face him, she slid her arms around his neck, drawing his mouth down to hers. "I missed you last night," she whispered against his lips, enjoying the feel of his hands tracing a pattern along her back to her hips, tightening his grip.

Linc groaned at the sound of the door opening, footsteps padding toward the bed.

"Oh no," Selena moaned, knowing she'd waited too long to slip out of bed and into her clothes. She buried her head in Linc's chest, wishing she could disappear.

"Dad? Is Selena still here?" Caid climbed up on Linc's side, resting his hands on his dad's shoulders and glancing over, a smile blossoming on his face. "Can we play ball again today, Selena?"

Linc's deep, husky laughter filled the room as she curled more tightly into him. "I think the secret is out, Selena. You might as well answer him."

She looked up, brushing strands of hair from her eyes as she focused on the eager face on the other side of Linc.

"Good morning, Caid."

"Can we?" he asked again, ignoring her greeting.

"Give her a minute to wake up, Caid," Linc admonished in a gentle tone. "How about you make us some coffee?"

Caid's mouth opened wide, his head shaking furiously. "I don't know how."

"Well, I guess it's time you learned. Come with me." He slid from the bed, wearing a pair of boxers and nothing else. Grabbing a pair of jeans, he slipped into them, leaving the top button loose as he set a hand on Caid's shoulder. "We men will go to the kitchen and give Selena time to get dressed. Okay?"

Caid looked over his shoulder at the bed, his expression growing serious as he nodded. "Okay, Dad."

******

"One more piece of bacon. Who wants it?" Linc nodded toward the plate in the center of the table.

"Me!" Caid leaned forward, grabbing it in a quick motion and taking a bite.

Selena sipped her coffee, watching Caid clean his plate. Her heart tripped over itself. She'd fallen in love with not only the man beside her, but his son, as well. The knowledge caused a series of emotions to pass through her. Vulnerability, excitement, fear, and hope all warred with each other to claim a prominent place in her mind. Here she was, acting as if she were a firm part of their lives, yet it wasn't true. Not once had Linc mentioned love or a future together. Their relationship was as tentative as it had been during their first week together.

Not until he'd gone silent for several days, during the problems at work and learning about Caid, did she accept how deeply she'd fallen for this man. Not for the first time, she thought of his comment a few days before, wondering if Linc felt the need to test the waters, see who best fit into his new life.

"Any relationship I pursue now becomes more complicated."

She might be reading too much into it, but she couldn't shake the need to protect herself and her heart. Until Linc expressed his feelings, giving her some clue of his intent, she felt compelled to put some distance between them.

"Mr. Caldwell?"

Nina's voice came from the front entry, jerking Selena to the present.

"We're in the kitchen, Nina." Linc stood, picking up the empty plates.

Selena stood, grabbing glasses and following him to the sink. "I'd better go."

Taking her hands in his, Linc studied her face, detecting something he couldn't quite define.

"Are you all right?"

"I'm fine," she lied. "At some point, I *do* have to get into the office and stop being a slacker. This morning is as good a time as any."

"You? A slacker? I don't think so." Linc chuckled at the ridiculous notion. She and her sisters worked as hard as any business owners to continue the success of the company their father had started.

Blushing at his obvious compliment, she pulled her hands from his. "Caly has decided to pick up some real estate clients, and I volunteered to help her get back into the groove of selling."

"Will she still be in charge of the property management clients?" He followed her to his bedroom, standing to one side as she picked up her purse, jacket, and a small bag he hadn't noticed until now.

"Yes. I think she feels the need to expand her skills, and her income. With sales, she'll be able to pocket a little more cash."

"What's that?" He nodded at the bag in her hand.

Biting her lower lip, she glanced up at him. "My extra clothes. I thought it would be best to take them back to my place. With Caid here…" She stopped when she saw the unmistakable look of disapproval on Linc's face. "What?"

He reached out, gripping the bag and taking it from her hand. "Those are going to stay right here. In fact, bring anything else you need for staying more than overnight." Tossing the bag into the closet, he closed the distance between them. "After this morning, I think Caid might be confused if you aren't here."

"If you're suggesting I move in, I can't. We're, well…you know."

"We're what, Selena?"

She shifted from one foot to the other, not wanting to get into this now.

Resting his hands on her shoulders, he pulled her to him, nibbling the corners of her mouth. "We're what?" he rasped out again, taking her mouth with his.

Leaning into him, she gripped his arms, holding him close as he continued his gentle, seductive kisses. The fact he could fog her mind with such little effort wasn't fair. Sighing against his lips, she pulled back, resting her forehead against his.

"Please, Linc. Let's not talk about this now."

His gaze roamed over her face, trying to decipher what was going through her mind. Usually, she wore her emotions so anyone could tell what she thought. Not this morning, however.

"Are you having second thoughts about us?"

"No, it's just…" Selena wasn't prepared to give him an explanation about what bothered her.

"I won't push. If you need time, more space, just tell me. I don't want you to feel trapped in a relationship with me." He swallowed the bitter taste of those words.

Placing a hand on his arm, she leaned up, kissing his cheek. "I don't feel trapped at all." She wanted to tell him her feelings, that she loved him, but now wasn't the time. "May I come back and make dinner for you?"

"As long as you plan to stay the night."

A small smile played on her lips. "I believe that can be arranged, Mr. Caldwell."

Wrapping his arms around her, he gave her one more heated kiss, then stepped back. "Good. As long as we're clear, Ms. Kerrigan."

Feeling her face heat, she turned, flashing him a glorious smile. "Oh, we're definitely clear."

******

"Selena, Chad Donovan is in the lobby. Do you have time to see him?"

Sighing, Selena leaned toward the speakerphone, wishing she had a legitimate excuse not to, like a pending appointment. She checked her calendar once more, hoping she'd missed something important. No such luck. "Yes, Tricia. Tell Mr. Donovan I'll be right out."

Standing, she straightened her skirt. Whatever he wanted, she'd keep it short, then send him on his way.

"Chad. It's good to see you again." Extending her hand, she held back a grimace when he took it, squeezing lightly.

"I'm glad you're here. I wondered if you might have time for lunch."

"I don't—"

"It's important, Selena."

If it weren't for the grave expression on his face, she'd have turned him down.

"I don't have much time before my next appointment."

"We'll make it quick. You pick the place." Chad shoved his hands in his pockets, glancing at Tricia behind the receptionist desk, noting her curious expression. "It's better we not talk here."

"All right. I'll let Tricia know, then get my purse."

Walking back to her office, she looked up in time to see Julia coming out of her own office.

"You look like you're in a hurry."

"Someone from my past showed up and wants to go to lunch. I don't have time, but…" She shrugged, not wanting to say more.

"Who?" Julia asked, glancing around her to get a look at the man standing in the lobby.

"Chad Donovan."

Groaning, Julia gripped her elbow, ushering Selena into an empty office and closing the door. "I'm so sorry. I should've warned you Chad was in Peregrine Bay."

Selena's brows shot up. "You knew?"

"I'd heard, but hadn't seen him. I meant to tell you, but so much has been happening between you and Linc, it slipped my mind. You know he's friends with Tom Harten."

"I saw the two of them together a few nights ago when Linc took me to dinner. It doesn't surprise me because Chad's brother and Tom were good friends in college. I saw the three of them hanging out on campus a few times." Selena crossed her arms, resting her hip against the desk. "I just don't know what he wants to see me about. He says it's important."

"A guess? He wants to talk with you about the arts center bid."

"In that case, this won't be a long lunch. I have no sway in that decision."

"Yes, but he wouldn't be here unless he suspected you might." Opening the door, she stepped aside. "Don't worry about it. Enjoy your lunch, then tell me all about it." Julia winked as Selena walked past.

Chapter Eighteen

"So tell me what's so important." Selena sipped her iced tea, wanting to make this meeting brief. She'd studied him as he ordered lunch. If anything, Chad had gotten more handsome over the years, maturing from a lean college student to a broad-shouldered, muscular adult. It didn't impress her. She'd already seen too much of his toned physique up close and personal.

Leaning forward, he rested his arms on the table. "Well, I mentioned that I work for my stepfather, Ephraim Simondson."

She held up her hand to stop him. "If this is about the arts center contract, I have absolutely no say in their decision. If you want to impress someone, you should be taking my sister, Julia, to lunch."

Chad laughed. "I can see I missed out in college by not getting to know you better, Selena."

"And what makes you think I would've been interested?" Her brow quirked up in question.

"Don't pretend you weren't attracted to me."

"That was a lifetime ago, Chad. I am way beyond college crushes."

"Touché." He picked up his drink, took a swallow, then set down the glass, his face turning serious. "Be careful of Linc Caldwell."

Her head jerked back. "Linc and I are none of your business, Chad. If that's why you asked me here, I might as well leave." She started to stand, stopping when he held up his hand.

"I'm sorry. I started this off wrong. Please, sit down, Selena."

She glanced around, cringing at the number of people looking in her direction. Plastering on a smile, she sat back down.

"All right. Why don't you start over?"

"You already know Caldwell's company and mine are battling for the arts center award."

"Of course."

"What you may not know is TSR has been experiencing serious breaches of their system, jeopardizing client data. I have reason to believe they're being less than honest with their clients about the extent of the attacks."

"In fact, I *do* know a little about what's happened. I can assure you, they'd never hide any kind of data loss from their clients. I've known Linc long enough to know that isn't the way they operate."

Chad leaned forward, his gaze boring into hers. "And have you known him long enough to be certain he isn't using you to get an inside path to the award?"

Anger flared, but she kept her seat, feeling the color drain from her face.

"I can see it has crossed your mind," he continued. "My guess is you're shoving your concerns aside, hoping his interest is in you and nothing else."

Selena swallowed the bile his words triggered, pushing down the doubt. Yes, she'd asked herself the same question when they first went out, wondering why someone like Linc would be attracted to a quiet, small town girl like her. His history had been to date women with a much higher profile, women the press would find newsworthy. Those women, along with the rapid success of TSR and Linc's enviable record as a SEAL team leader, captured media attention and sold magazines. The over-the-top social media reach of his dating history didn't hurt awareness of him or his company, and she could only imagine what it did for the women.

"This has nothing to do with my interest in the award. My concern is for you, Selena. If you're anything like you were in college, you're still a nice, albeit naïve, woman. And probably still much too trusting."

Her eyes widened, her lips parting at the brash comment. "Are you referring to the party?"

"What else?" A cocky grin split his face. "Did you think I didn't know you wandered into the shoot that night? I'm certain you got an eyeful."

Tossing down her napkin, she leaned toward him, her voice low. "This conversation is over. From now on, if you want to talk about the arts center bid or Linc Caldwell, I suggest you take it up with Julia or the mayor. Or even your good friend, Tom Harten. Both subjects are off limits with me."

"Selena, wait."

"No, you wait. You set me up that night, and you're trying to mess with my head again today. I'll have none of it. I'm not in college any longer, and in case you haven't noticed, Peregrine Bay is *my* turf, not yours. You won't be able to get away with the same shoddy actions you pulled before. Good luck on the bid. If today's conversation provides any clue, you'll need it."

Ignoring the curious stares of other diners, she kept her expression neutral, squared her shoulders, and walked outside. As the door closed behind her, she let out a deep, exasperated breath. Instead of walking toward the office, she headed in the opposite direction, toward the park on the water. Hearing her phone, she reached into her purse. Linc. A sick feeling spread through her.

She hated Chad's insinuation. Worse, she hated the fact she'd harbored the same concern.

Nodding absently as she passed people she knew, Selena found herself standing near the water, a few feet from the bench where she and Linc had talked the day he'd returned her missing sandals. The memory felt bittersweet. Rational thought told her to heed her own doubts and Chad's warning about Linc's true intentions. Her heart schooled her otherwise. Which to believe?

Picking up a small, flat stone, she skipped it across the water, recalling the day her father had shown her his technique at the lake behind their home. She'd practiced diligently for weeks, perfecting her throw. A small achievement, yet doing it right had meant a great deal to her at the time.

All her life she'd worked hard to do everything right, avoiding mistakes and not embarrassing herself or her family. Not because her father had issued any type of warning, but because doing things right was part of her character, a source of pride, defining her as a person. When Chad invited her to the party in college, she hadn't made the right decision. What made her think his guidance today would be of any value?

Wrapping her arms around her waist, she took a seat on the bench, ignoring another call from Linc. She'd speak with him later, once she felt in control of her emotions. For the umpteenth time, Selena wished she could be more like Caly. Her younger sister had the ability to take life moment by moment, enjoying each minute without regret. If decisions worked out, fine. If not, there was always tomorrow.

But she wasn't like Caly. Not even close. She tended to worry over her choices, careful to consider every option before committing. With Linc, she hadn't allowed herself time to think through the reasons for his interest. Her attraction to him had been immediate and overwhelming, flooding her senses with emotions she'd never felt for another man. In hindsight, it had been stupid to rush into a relationship with him—assuming that's what this was—without understanding why a man such as Linc would find her interesting enough to continue seeing.

Selena knew men found her attractive and seemed to enjoy her company. Then the tenuous connection would fade away, like a fog bank dissipating before your eyes. Nothing had ever lasted. She had to admit, most of it had been her fault. No one had held her interest for more than a few dates.

Her phone rang again. Checking it, she saw Linc's image for the third time in less than two hours. She let her finger hover over the answer button before touching it.

"Hi, Linc."

"I've been trying to reach you. Is everything all right?"

She'd asked herself the same question several times since seeing Chad. "Yes, everything is fine. I've been busy trying to catch up after taking those days off. Why?"

"I'm back at the office. We're experiencing another attempted attack on our system." When he paused, she could hear voices in the background. "I have no idea when I'll be home, so don't worry about tonight. I'll ask Nina to fix dinner for Caid."

Selena could hear what sounded like a combination of worry and resolve. He'd take care of what needed to be done at work, but his new parental responsibilities added another layer onto his already hectic life. At least she could do something to relieve part of the burden.

"Nonsense. I'll stop by my place and change, then drive to your house. I should be there by five. Can you let Nina know?" she asked, pushing aside her doubts.

"Are you sure?" The relief in his voice touched her.

"Absolutely. Take care of business and get home when you can. Caid and I will be fine."

"That's great, Selena. I'll call Nina…" He paused, as if he had more to say, but finished with a simple goodbye. "See you later."

He hung up before she had a chance to say anything else, which was for the best. What she wanted to say had to take place in person, not over the phone while he scrambled to deal with one more threat to TSR.

Pushing up from the bench, she took one more look across the lake as a flight of ducks landed a hundred yards away. She wondered at the energy it took to migrate hundreds of miles, then embark on a return flight. Unlike humans, their life patterns were predetermined at birth. They didn't wrestle with what ifs or doubts, like she was doing now.

Straightening her shoulders, Selena considered her two choices. One, ask Linc straight out if he saw a future for them, bracing herself for his response. Or two, take each day as it came, enjoy their time together, and not worry about her own doubts. Neither choice protected her from potential heartache, but instinct told her to go with what felt right.

Relationships didn't run on a schedule and she had no intention of imposing one. She'd stop overthinking and start enjoying her time with Linc, just as she had the first few weeks. Other than the introduction of Caid into Linc's life, nothing had changed. Already having grown to love Caid as much as she loved his father, she prayed they'd feel the same about her someday.

******

"Phase three is active, C. It's time for you to make more anonymous calls to alert TSR clients about a possible breach of their data files. This one should shake them up the way your stepfather expects."

C felt a trace of regret at the chaos Rave was creating. Through no fault of their own, his actions would undermine

TSR's success, perhaps cause the loss of tens of thousands of dollars in business, and impact client retention. Ephraim's threats made it clear there'd been no choice, but C didn't have to like it.

"Thanks, Rave. I'll make the calls, then contact Ephraim. Knowing him, he'll waste no time contacting companies who selected TSR over Simondson to discover their current satisfaction level."

"This should get him off your back for a while." *Longer than a while if the results of the extra work ends as I hope*, Rave thought. "Let me know if you need anything else."

******

"Client calls are escalating to a critical level, Linc. Tina is working with our customer service crew so each employee provides an accurate and consistent message." Shane checked the status of the latest incident on his computer. "According to Vega, this attack is different from the last two." He glanced over his shoulder, his mouth twisting into a smirk. "It wasn't hard to convince him to work with Westfall on this one."

"Here's the latest." Matt handed Linc an updated report.

Linc didn't glance away from the spreadsheet as he studied the information. "This says no client data has been compromised. Can we rely on this, Matt?"

"It's the best information we have right now, and it's what Tina is telling the clients."

"Has Vega given you any idea on when this will be contained?"

"They've been working nonstop since he detected the breach. He and—"

"Hold on, guys," Shane interrupted. "Vega wants a conference call with us and Westfall. They've got some new Intel for us."

"Go ahead." Linc pulled up a chair. "We're here, Vega. What do you have for us?"

"I didn't want to say anything until I checked all the data, but I've discovered where the attacks are originating."

The door swung open as Tina entered. Linc motioned for her to grab a chair.

"Tina just joined us, Vega. Go ahead."

"At first, given the sophistication of the attacks, I didn't believe what I was finding. It was as if whoever set this up was leading me to the source."

Linc noticed Tina's eyes widen as she bit her bottom lip.

"Details, Vega," Linc prompted, growing impatient.

"Right. After being routed to China and back, I found the first incident came from the northwest area, but I could never get the source. The second incident went cold at a public location in Oregon. The third attack led us to gold."

"Vega..." Linc's voice turned to hard frustration.

"Got it, boss. I hope you're all sitting down because you aren't going to believe this. From what I can tell, this latest threat, and probably the others, came from an address in Portland. I don't yet have a name, but if I were a betting man, which I am, I'd say our friendly competitor is out to get us."

"Simondson?" Linc asked, the pulse point in his jaw twitching.

"Appears so. Give me a couple more hours, but if you know anyone in law enforcement, you may want to give them a heads-up."

******

"Open up, Donovan. We need to talk." Linc pounded on the motel room door, Matt and Shane behind him doing their best to calm him down. He slammed his fist on the door again. "Donovan…open up."

They stepped back as the door slowly opened, a bleary-eyed Chad Donovan standing there. When he saw them, his eyes went wide.

"What the hell do you guys want?" He stood before them in his underwear, the television blaring in the background.

"A little early to sack out, isn't it? Or have you been prematurely celebrating?" Linc pushed past him, ignoring Chad's protests.

"When I sack out is no business of yours." His mind slowly cleared, a smirk forming on his face. "Celebrating what? Ah…they must've awarded the arts center contract. My guess is TSR didn't get it."

Matt and Shane walked inside, closing the door behind them.

"No, it hasn't been awarded yet, but I'm relatively certain who is going to get it." Linc swiped magazines off a chair and onto the floor, taking a seat, looking around the clean, cheap motel room. "This the best Ephraim can do?"

Chad grabbed a pair of jeans, pulling them on, glaring down at Linc. "Look, I don't know why the hell you're here, but you apparently think it's good enough to barge in and ruin my sleep. Why don't you give me a clue?"

"Did you and your stepfather honestly believe you could set us up, hack our system, then send warning messages to clients without us detecting the source?" Linc kept his voice low, absently drawing circles on the table next to him. He glanced up, his gaze feral. "You think you could break into our system with so little effort?"

Chad blanched, expelling a deep breath, his arms limp at his sides. "Look, Caldwell, I don't know what you're talking about. I haven't spoken to my stepfather in a week, and he definitely doesn't trust me to handle anything beyond a meet-and-greet. If there's more to this, you'd better enlighten me."

Linc, Matt, and Shane exchanged looks, wondering if Chad hadn't been dialed-in on the happenings at TSR.

"Are you telling us you have no idea about the attempts Simondson has made to hack our system, steal client data, and gather company secrets?" Linc stood, stepping to within a foot of Chad.

"No shit? Ephraim actually tried something that stupid." He scrubbed a hand down his face, shaking his head. "I'll be damned. He must be getting desperate. Tell me more about what happened." He lowered himself to the bed, resting his arms on his knees, seeing the surprise on Linc's face.

"I'll share what we know, but believe me, Donovan, if you're involved at all, you *will* go down."

******

"I hate to say it, but I don't think Donovan is involved." Matt slid into Linc's truck, glancing back at the door to Chad's room.

"I agree, Linc. Something isn't right about all this. He seemed too happy about his stepdad crossing the line and getting caught. Appears there's bad blood between those two." Shane shut the door as Linc started the engine.

"If not Chad, then who?" Linc asked. "Ephraim sent him here to push votes toward Simondson and secure the contract. Is there somebody else we don't know about?"

"Hey, it doesn't take a local person to do what they did. The hacker could be located anywhere," Matt offered.

Linc pinched the bridge of his nose. "I suppose you're right. Guess we'll know more after we get law enforcement involved. I'll call Adam Monroe in the morning, get an investigation started."

"Whatever the outcome, I'm pretty certain Chad won't be employed by his stepdad much longer." Shane grinned at the thought.

"I don't expect anyone at that company will be employed once this is made public." Linc shook his head.

"Greed, ego, and stupid decisions. It's a dangerous trifecta, gentlemen."

Chapter Nineteen

"When will my dad be back?" Caid yawned again, as he had many times while trying to stay awake until Linc returned.

"He might not be back tonight, sweetie." Selena tucked the covers around him, then swiped a strand of hair, so much like his father's, from his forehead. "I'm sure he'll be here as soon as he can."

Caid stared at her, his piercing blue eyes narrowing.

"What is it?" Selena asked, seeing the question on his face.

"Do you think he's my *real* dad?" For such a quiet voice, it carried a major impact.

She sucked in a breath. Caid had been referring to Linc as dad or daddy. Selena assumed they had this discussion before now, but given the circumstances and all the issues at work, she could see how Linc had put it off.

"You mean Linc?" She wanted to stall for time, give herself a moment to think of a good response.

Caid nodded, his gaze fixed on her as if she held the answer to the biggest question in his world.

"You'll need to ask Linc, sweetie." Selena could tell it wasn't the answer Caid wanted when his eyes lost some of their spark. He slipped further under the covers, as if trying to hide his disappointment. His world had been rocked twice in his short life. At six years old, he needed to know where he belonged and if Linc would stick around.

Linc came to an abrupt stop outside Caid's bedroom, his jacket in one hand, his other hand reaching toward the door before he pushed it open. The question his son asked pierced his chest.

He'd never thought of clarifying his answer, telling Caid that yes, he was his *real* father. Their first encounter had almost been too easy, two friends playing on the floor with a bag full of action figures. When Caid asked if Linc would be his daddy, he'd given the most natural response—yes. They'd never spoken of it again.

Linc wondered if Selena weren't here tonight, would Caid have asked him directly, or would he have let himself worry about it, creating confusion and uncertainty.

"Hey, buddy." Linc pushed the door open, tossing his jacket aside as Caid came fully awake.

"Dad!" He launched himself into Linc's outstretched arms.

"I hope you were good for Selena."

Caid nodded, looking at Selena over Linc's shoulder, a contented smile on his face.

"What did you two do?"

"We played ball, ate hamburgers, played video games." He looked at Selena.

"Drove to Pine Cove for ice cream." Selena smiled at the big grin on Caid's face.

"I got chocolate."

Link's eyes widened. "Chocolate, huh? And all I've had since breakfast is an energy bar and coffee."

Selena placed a hand on Linc's shoulder. "I'll go make something while you and Caid talk."

"No, stay. I can eat later."

Her gaze shot from Linc to Caid, who still had his arms wrapped around his father's neck.

"You know where to find me. Just follow the smell of grilled cheese." She walked out, closing the door behind her.

******

As two sandwiches grilled on the stove, Selena wrapped the remaining block of cheddar cheese, setting it in the refrigerator. Picking up a cup of coffee, she waited, hearing the sound of a door closing down the hall. A moment later, Linc walked into the kitchen, his face haggard but at peace.

"He missed you." She poured him some coffee as he sat, handing it to him before returning to the stove. Taking down a plate, she scooped up the sandwiches. "Here. You look like you need food."

Snaking an arm around her waist, he pulled Selena onto his lap, nuzzling her neck with his lips. "What I need is bed…and you."

She laughed, pulling back and picking up a sandwich. "I think we can make that work. First, you need to eat." Holding it to his mouth, she laughed at the disappointed look on his face.

Finishing the first sandwich in record time, he shoved the plate away, turning Selena so she straddled his lap. Shredding his hands into her hair, he pulled her down, nibbling at her lips before settling his mouth over hers.

Her eyes closed as she slid her hands to this shoulders, then wrapped them around the back of his neck. Lacing her fingers through his hair, she moaned softly, hungry for his taste, his touch. Fire streaked through her as he deepened the kiss, moving against her, creating a heat almost unbearable in its intensity.

Shifting, Linc moved his hands to her hips, lightly massaging as his mouth worked its magic on hers. Blood pounded through his body as a fire he'd never known blazed through him. He couldn't get enough of her…would never get enough of her. A hungry growl escaped his lips as his tongue collided with hers, tangling, retreating, then plunging in again. He could feel his heart thundering as his hands moved to her thighs before sliding under the hem of her blouse.

Breaking the kiss, he pulled back, his breathing ragged, a heated glare in his eyes. Desire speared deep in his belly as he saw yearning as strong as his own in her eyes.

"I need you, Selena." Standing, he held her steady, tightening his hold. "Wrap your legs around me," he breathed out, taking her mouth again, walking into his bedroom and pushing the door closed.

******

"Caid only said *okay*," Linc chuckled, his fingers grazing up and down Selena's arm as they lay in bed, morning sun streaming through the parted curtains.

"He didn't ask any questions? Seems you got off much too easy." She smiled against his chest, her fingers playing with the silken hairs.

"That so?" Linc laughed, although he felt the same. "He asked if I was his real daddy, and I said yes." He glanced down at her, enjoying the way her fingers played against his body. "Real men don't need a lot of words."

This time, Selena laughed. "I'm beginning to understand that. Other than my father and cousins, I haven't spent much time around *real* men." She tugged lightly on his chest hair.

"Ow," he muttered, then flipped her on top so she straddled his waist. "You play dirty, Ms. Kerrigan."

"You have no idea, Mr. Caldwell." A wicked smile crossed her face.

He splayed his hands across her back, drawing her down for a kiss. "Show me," he whispered against her lips.

"Now?" she breathed back.

"Oh, yeah," he groaned, tightening his hold as he hardened beneath her.

******

"I'd appreciate it, Adam. We have a lot of data to give them, and we'll do whatever is needed to get this resolved." Linc held the phone to his ear, resting a shoulder against the patio door, watching Selena show Caid how to throw a Frisbee.

A week had passed since Vega and Westfall discovered the data needed to identify the source of their problems. Adam was more than willing to help nail the man.

"Yes, we can set up a meeting to hand off the data. Let me know when and where. And, Adam, I'd prefer you be present," Linc said. He hung up, then dialed another number. "Matt, I want the group brought together at eleven this morning. Adam Monroe has assured the FBI we have what is needed and they want to see us sooner rather than later. We'll go over what we have and pull together any other data they may find useful. Vega and Westfall should conference in."

"Vega can conference. Westfall flew into Spokane this morning. He's driving over now."

"I'll be there in thirty minutes, Matt." He hung up, more than ready to turn everything over to the FBI.

"Are you off again?" Selena walked up to him, sliding her arms around his neck, placing a soft kiss on his lips.

"I've called the team together for a brief meeting. It shouldn't take long, but I know you need to get some work done. Nina is on her way. Can you stay until she gets here?" He returned the kiss, glancing over her shoulder at Caid, who worked on figuring out the Frisbee.

"Of course. I don't have any appointments, so I may work from home."

"Perfect. I'll swing by after the meeting and take you to a late lunch. By the water, if that's okay." Linc stroked a finger down her cheek. He needed to make a quick stop in Pine Cove before picking Selena up, then he wanted some time alone with her.

"Sounds wonderful. Casual, I hope."

"Absolutely."

******

"I believe we've covered everything. Each of you has a job to do before we compile the final report for the FBI. Unless you need to confirm some data, don't put in any more hours on this, other than preparing the reports. Adam assures me the FBI will want to confirm what we provide, so they'll be putting some time into this." Linc looked around the room at each person who'd helped close out the latest round of threats. "Look, people, I don't know where this is going. As we've discussed before, the person we thought helped Simondson doesn't seem to know anything about the hacking. My gut tells me someone else, maybe even someone close to us, is involved, but that's all I have to go on. Instinct. Keep vigilant." Taking a breath, he stood. "I want to thank each one of you. Without your dedication and extra effort, we might still be mired in this mess. Following where the data led, not giving up, everything you did was critical."

"And we can't overlook the work Tina did, taking care of our clients." Matt glanced at her, seeing her face color a rosy red, her gaze focused on the floor. "We didn't lose a single one, Tina. Thank you."

"I'm glad I could do my part." Tina scooted her chair back, putting distance between her and the others, not looking up.

"You did more than that, and it won't go unnoticed," Linc added.

She nodded, staying silent.

"I don't believe we've ever been properly introduced." Gray glanced toward Tina, extending his hand. "Gray Westfall."

"It's very nice to meet you. I'm Tina."

"I have a good friend back home named Tina. A nickname, I think," Gray added.

"Actually, Christina is my legal name. Most people call me Tina, but close friends just call me C."

******

Linc couldn't get Tina's odd reaction to their compliments out of his mind as he left Pine Cove. She'd exhibited strength and confidence during the recent crisis. Today, her actions indicated a woman who wanted to be anywhere else except in a room accepting congratulations.

He thought on it a few more minutes, reaching no answers. Linc decided he wouldn't spend any more time on the Tina mystery—at least not today. Answers eventually came out. Patience had its advantages.

Pulling into Selena's driveway, he vowed to focus on her for the remainder of the afternoon. Other than Caid, she'd become the most important person in his life, burrowing under his skin and into his heart. Surprisingly, the extent of the love he had for her didn't bother him as much as he'd always thought it would. All he had to do now was convince her of his feelings and hope she felt the same.

"Hey. You're here earlier than I expected." Selena opened the door, stepping outside. Locking the door, she moved into his open arms, accepting the kiss he offered. "Hmmm, that's the best greeting I've ever had."

His gaze wandered over her, unfamiliar fear flashing through him. Clearing his throat, he threaded his fingers through hers. "You hungry?"

"Starving."

He tightened his grip before letting go to open the car door. "Good. I have a place in mind."

They drove in silence, Linc glancing at Selena more than once, seeing her relaxed.

"It's been a hectic few weeks." His deep voice sounded unsteady, hesitant, as if he were searching for something to say.

Selena tilted her head, studying his face. Reaching over, she rested a hand on his thigh. "Is everything all right?"

Looking down, he placed his hand over hers. "Yeah, everything's fine. I'm just glad we've identified the source of the hacking." He did feel fine, other than the lump in his throat and tightness in his chest.

She shrugged, taking him at his word. He'd get around to telling her what bothered him on his own time. Pushing would do nothing but make it worse.

Pulling into a parking place at a lakefront restaurant, he killed the engine. Walking around the car, he opened her door.

"Come on. Let's eat, then take a walk." He held out a hand, helping her out, then slipped an arm around her shoulders.

******

The table by a window, having a beautiful view of the lake, created a wonderful atmosphere. Selena tried to relax, devouring her vegetables with pasta while Linc finished off a hamburger with all the trimmings. Reaching across the table, she snagged a french fry, popped it into her mouth, then took another.

Linc pushed the plate toward her and sat back. "Go for it. I'm too stuffed to eat any more."

He'd said little on the drive and less at the restaurant. Maybe the reality of becoming a father had finally settled in, causing him to rethink the rest of his life, including the people in it. Again, she pushed aside the uneasy feeling in her stomach, deciding to enjoy their time together.

"How about a walk?" Linc stood, pulling out her chair, taking her hand. "I need to get some air."

They strolled along the water's edge, Linc clutching her hand as if it were a lifeline. From this location, he could see the spot where, two months prior, he and Selena had their first real conversation. The day he'd made the decision she was much too good to let go.

He'd tired of the single life, dating strictly to get out and away from his work. An inner voice told him Selena offered more, and he wanted it, wanted her. The doubts he'd felt over the last few weeks had more to do with his blundered first marriage than his feelings for Selena. He and Valerie had jumped into marriage after a couple weeks. It had never felt quite right, yet he'd gone ahead. If it weren't for Caid, he would've considered the brief union a total failure.

"Oh, look." Selena pointed toward the lake where several geese swam in the cool water. "I thought they'd all be further south by now."

"There always seems to be a few stragglers." Turning, he spotted an empty bench a few feet away. "Why don't we sit and watch them?"

The minutes ticked by, neither speaking as the sun warmed their faces. Linc blew out a shaky breath, shifting on the bench to look at Selena. Brushing a strand of hair from her face, he leaned over, brushing a kiss across her temple.

"I know my life has been out of control the last few weeks. It hasn't given us much time alone."

Her eyes crinkled as a grin lifted the corners of her mouth. "I don't mind. What time we've had has been good, don't you think?"

"Yes, it's been better than good. The weeks with you have been the best of my life." He could feel her body shift toward him. "I know I've said this before, but Valerie and I weren't in love. Lust, perhaps, but that's a faint comparison to what I feel for you, Selena."

Her lips parted, her eyes growing wide as she sucked in a breath.

"The first week we were together, I knew how I felt. I've held it in, not saying a word, hoping you'd come to feel the same. It's no longer in me to keep silent." He knelt before her. "This may be too soon for you. If it is, I'll accept it and we'll go on from there." Taking her hands, he kissed her knuckles, then turned them over, placing warm kisses on her wrists and her palms. Glancing up, he noticed moisture in her eyes. "I love you, Selena. I've never said that to a woman before. I'll do whatever is needed to keep you in my life. Tell me what you want, what will make you happy, and I'll do my best to make it happen."

Pulling a hand free, she placed it over her mouth, tears glistening on her face. "You, Linc. You're all I want."

He closed his eyes in relief and reached into his pocket. "Marry me, Selena. You, Caid, and I will build a life like no other. We'll create our own kind of love unlike any other." He opened his hand, revealing a stunning diamond and ruby ring.

Blinking rapidly, trying to swipe tears from her face, she nodded.

"Is that a yes?" he chuckled, although the knot in his gut still tugged at him.

"Yes, and yes again. I love you, Linc. I have since the day you walked into my office, my sandals in your hand, and asked if I was Cinderella. Today, I believe I am."

Epilogue

Three months later…

"Stand still, Selena. I'll never get this veil on right if you keep moving." Julia grabbed another clip, adjusting it until she felt satisfied it would hold. "There. Now you can move."

Selena stood in front of the mirror, still not quite believing within an hour she'd be Mrs. Lincoln Caldwell. The thought still sent shivers through her body, the same as every time Linc touched her.

"Oh my." Caly stood at the window, pulling back the curtain to stare toward the lawn where wedding guests were taking their seats.

"What is it?" Julia asked, walking up beside her.

"More like *who*. Right there, standing next to Linc's parents." Caly nodded toward a man in military uniform, awards on his left breast, a beret on his head. "Wow. Who invited him?"

"All right. Now you've gotten my interest." Selena joined them, poking her head between the two, looking in the direction they were staring. She bit back a smile when she recognized the officer from a photo in Linc's study. The picture showed Linc's older brother wearing a West Point uniform, a stern expression on a handsome, uncompromising face. The man outside had more creases, a deeper tan, and stood well over six feet tall.

"That is one hot piece of male," Caly breathed out, a hand coming to her throat.

Julia burst out laughing, raising a hand to press it against her sister's forehead. "Are you all right? I've never heard you react like this to any man."

Caly brushed Julia's hand away, her expression turning to indignation. "That's because I've never seen one as fine as that one." She looked at Selena, then took another look outside. "Okay, spill it. Who is he?"

"If I'm not mistaken, he's Linc's brother, Dez." Selena was as surprised as Julia at Caly's reaction. "Linc asked him to be his best man, but when he didn't show for the rehearsal dinner, we figured he couldn't make it."

"Well, he's here now." She made a show of fanning her face. "Excuse me, ladies. I think one of us should give him a formal Kerrigan welcome." Caly dashed out of the room before either could respond.

Julia cocked her head, then looked at Selena before they both started laughing.

"I never thought I'd live to see the day Caly reacted that way." Julia turned back to the window. "Is he single, or is she in for a broken heart before she's even met the man?"

"According to Linc, he's single—and a confirmed bachelor. I believe Linc said something to the effect the Army is his only love." Selena shrugged, not quite understanding the uncompromising connection some people made with their career in the military.

"There's the minister. Looks like it's time for this show to start." Julia kissed Selena on the cheek. "I'll send Dad to the foyer. Love you, Selena."

"Love you, too, Julia."

******

Holding a flute of champagne, Selena still had the broad smile she'd worn when walking down the aisle toward Linc. It had been an hour. She couldn't seem to come down from the high.

"Are you all right?" Linc slid an arm around her waist, brushing a kiss against her neck.

"More than all right." She rested her head on his shoulder, unable to suppress a sigh. "I can't believe the changes to my life in less than six months."

His deep, throaty laugh had her drawing away and looking up at him. "All for the better, I hope."

"I couldn't ask for more." She scanned the crowd, seeing her youngest sisters, Danielle and Lillian, talking with several of their friends, and spotting Caid running around with a group of children. "I'm so glad Dez made it."

"He's a hard man to pin down, although it appears Caly is doing her best to do just that." He nodded toward the dance floor they'd set up in front of the band where Caly and Dez danced together. "She sure doesn't waste time."

"You may need to warn her off. I don't want to see her get hurt." Selena watched the expression on her sister's face as she danced with Dez. "I've never seen her act like this."

"I don't think you have anything to worry about. Dez and my parents leave in two days. If history repeats itself, I won't see him again for a couple years." Linc's voice signaled his disappointment at not having more time with his brother.

"We can always go visit him."

Linc's brows drew together. "He has no real home, Selena. Wherever the Army sends him is his home. We have to wait for him to come to us."

"We wondered where you went, old man." Matt clasped Linc on the shoulder as Shane, his girlfriend, and Linc's closest colleagues at TSR formed a circle around the couple.

Linc reached out, shaking hands with Tomás Vega, then Gray Westfall. "Good to see you all made it."

"Hey, we wouldn't have missed it. Besides, there are many reasons to celebrate." Shane slung an arm over his girlfriend's shoulder.

"The work is underway at the arts center, we've had no hacking attempts in three months, and Ephraim Simondson has charges pending against him and his company. Adam's friends at the FBI say they have more evidence than needed to smack him with jail time and a huge fine." Matt sent a look at Vega and Westfall.

"The idiot didn't know whoever he hired to sabotage us was either incompetent or a complete genius. No one could miss the trail right back to Simondson servers." Vega brought his glass of beer up, taking a long swallow. "Too bad Tina took a job back east. She seemed to be the perfect fit to handle client communications."

Linc agreed, believing there was more to her leaving TSR than the job offer which had come out of nowhere. Maybe he'd get answers someday, maybe not. Today, he had everything he wanted.

"Come on, guys. I'm in the mood to dance, and I'm sure these two want a few minutes alone." Shane took his girlfriend's hand, leading her toward the dance floor.

Selena's gaze followed them, searching for any sign of Caly or Dez. Not seeing either, she shot a look at Linc.

"Have you seen Dez or Caly lately?"

"They walked toward the bar a few minutes ago." Linc settled a hand on Selena's back, scanning the crowd. "I'll be damned," he muttered, not sure if what he saw should be shared with his bride.

"What? Can you see them?"

He cleared his throat, nodding toward the line of parked cars. Dez and Caly were wrapped around each other, giving the guests a real show.

"Oh no. I'd better go warn her off." Selena started to walk away before Linc grabbed her arm, pulling her back.

"She's a big girl, and Dez is a big boy."

"But…" Her voice faded as Dez opened the door to a magnificent Lamborghini, holding it wide as Caly slid inside. Regardless of the joy she felt, her heart sank. Wherever Caly and Dez were off to, Selena knew, deep in her heart, her sister would never be the same.

Thank you for taking the time to read Our Kind of Love. If you enjoyed it, please consider telling your friends or posting a short review. Word of mouth is an author's best friend and much appreciated.

Please join my reader's group to be notified of my New Releases at: http://www.shirleendavies.com/contact-me.html

I care about quality, so if you find something in error, please contact me via email at shirleen@shirleendavies.com

About the Author

Shirleen Davies writes romance—historical, contemporary, and romantic suspense. She grew up in Southern California, attended Oregon State University, and has degrees from San Diego State University and the University of Maryland. During the day she provides consulting services to small and mid-sized businesses. But her real passion is writing emotionally charged stories of flawed people who find redemption through love and acceptance. She now lives with her husband in a beautiful town in northern Arizona.

Shirleen loves to hear from her readers.

Write to her at: shirleen@shirleendavies.com
Visit her website: http://www.shirleendavies.com
Sign up to be notified of New Releases:
http://www.shirleendavies.com/contact-me.html
Books by Shirleen:
http://www.shirleendavies.com/books.html
Comment on her blog:
http://www.shirleendavies.com/blog.html
Facebook Fan Page:
https://www.facebook.com/ShirleenDaviesAuthor
Twitter: http://twitter.com/shirleendavies
Google+: http://www.gplusid.com/shirleendavies
LinkedIn: http://www.linkedin.com/in/shirleendaviesauthor
Pinterest: http://www.pinterest.com/shirleendavies
Tsu: http://www.tsu.co/shirleendavies

Other Books by Shirleen Davies

Tougher than the Rest – Book One
MacLarens of Fire Mountain Historical Western Romance Series
"A passionate, fast-paced story set in the untamed western frontier by an exciting new voice in historical romance."

Niall MacLaren is the oldest of four brothers, and the undisputed leader of the family. A widower, and single father, his focus is on building the MacLaren ranch into the largest and most successful in northern Arizona. He is serious about two things—his responsibility to the family and his future marriage to the wealthy, well-connected widow who will secure his place in the territory's destiny.

Katherine is determined to live the life she's dreamed about. With a job waiting for her in the growing town of Los Angeles, California, the young teacher from Philadelphia begins a journey across the United States with only a couple of trunks and her spinster companion. Life is perfect for this adventurous, beautiful young woman, until an accident throws her into the arms of the one man who can destroy it all.

Fighting his growing attraction and strong desire for the beautiful stranger, Niall is more determined than ever to push emotions aside to focus on his goals of wealth and political gain. But looking into the clear, blue eyes of the woman who could ruin everything, Niall discovers he will have to harden his heart and be tougher than he's ever been in his life...Tougher than the Rest.

Faster than the Rest – Book Two

MacLarens of Fire Mountain Historical Western Romance Series

"Headstrong, brash, confident, and complex, the MacLarens of Fire Mountain will captivate you with strong characters set in the wild and rugged western frontier."

Handsome, ruthless, young U.S. Marshal Jamie MacLaren had lost everything—his parents, his family connections, and his childhood sweetheart—but now he's back in Fire Mountain and ready for another chance. Just as he successfully reconnects with his family and starts to rebuild his life, he gets the unexpected and unwanted assignment of rescuing the woman who broke his heart.

Beautiful, wealthy Victoria Wicklin chose money and power over love, but is now fighting for her life—or is she? Who has she become in the seven years since she left Fire Mountain to take up her life in San Francisco? Is she really as innocent as she says?

Marshal MacLaren struggles to learn the truth and do his job, but the past and present lead him in different directions as his heart and brain wage battle. Is Victoria a victim or a villain? Is life offering him another chance, or just another heartbreak?

As Jamie and Victoria struggle to uncover past secrets and come to grips with their shared passion, another danger arises. A life-altering danger that is out of their control and threatens to destroy any chance for a shared future.

Harder than the Rest – Book Three

MacLarens of Fire Mountain Historical Western Romance Series

"They are men you want on your side. Hard, confident, and loyal, the MacLarens of Fire

Mountain will seize your attention from the first page.”

Will MacLaren is a hardened, plain-speaking bounty hunter. His life centers on finding men guilty of horrendous crimes and making sure justice is done. There is no place in his world for the carefree attitude he carried years before when a tragic event destroyed his dreams.

Amanda is the daughter of a successful Colorado rancher. Determined and proud, she works hard to prove she is as capable as any man and worthy to be her father's heir. When a stranger arrives, her independent nature collides with the strong pull toward the handsome ranch hand. But is he what he seems and could his secrets endanger her as well as her family?

The last thing Will needs is to feel passion for another woman. But Amanda elicits feelings he thought were long buried. Can Will's desire for her change him? Or will the vengeance he seeks against the one man he wants to destroy—a dangerous opponent without a conscious—continue to control his life?

Stronger than the Rest – Book Four
MacLarens of Fire Mountain Historical Western Romance Series

“Smart, tough, and capable, the MacLarens protect their own no matter the odds. Set against America's rugged frontier, the stories of the men from Fire Mountain are complex, fast-paced, and a must read for anyone who enjoys non-stop action and romance.”

Drew MacLaren is focused and strong. He has achieved all of his goals except one—to return to the MacLaren ranch and build the best horse breeding program in the west. His successful career as an attorney is about to give way to his ranching roots when a bullet changes everything.

Tess Taylor is the quiet, serious daughter of a Colorado ranch family with dreams of her own. Her shy nature keeps her from developing friendships outside of her close-knit family until Drew enters her life. Their relationship grows. Then a bullet, meant for another, leaves him paralyzed and determined to distance himself from the one woman he's come to love.

Convinced he is no longer the man Tess needs, Drew focuses on regaining the use of his legs and recapturing a life he thought lost. But danger of another kind threatens those he cares about—including Tess—forcing him to rethink his future.

Can Drew overcome the barriers that stand between him, the safety of his friends and family, and a life with the woman he loves? To do it all, he has to be strong. Stronger than the Rest.

Deadlier than the Rest – Book Five
MacLarens of Fire Mountain Historical Western Romance Series

"A passionate, heartwarming story of the iconic MacLarens of Fire Mountain. This captivating historical western romance grabs your attention from the start with an engrossing story encompassing two romances set against the rugged backdrop of the burgeoning western frontier."

Connor MacLaren's search has already stolen eight years of his life. Now he is close to finding what he seeks—Meggie, his missing sister. His quest leads him to the growing city of Salt Lake and an encounter with the most captivating woman he has ever met.

Grace is the third wife of a Mormon farmer, forced into a life far different from what she'd have chosen. Her independent spirit longs for choices governed only by her own heart and mind. To achieve her dreams, she must hide behind secrets and half-truths, even as her heart pulls her towards the ruggedly handsome Connor.

Known as cool and uncompromising, Connor MacLaren lives by a few, firm rules that have served him well and kept him alive. However, danger stalks Connor, even to the front range of the beautiful Wasatch Mountains, threatening those he cares about and impacting his ability to find his sister.

Can Connor protect himself from those who seek his death? Will his eight-year search lead him to his sister while unlocking the secrets he knows are held tight within Grace, the woman who has captured his heart?

Read this heartening story of duty, honor, passion, and love in book five of the MacLarens of Fire Mountain series.

Wilder than the Rest – Book Six
MacLarens of Fire Mountain Historical Western Romance Series
"A captivating historical western romance set in the burgeoning and treacherous city of San Francisco. Go along for the ride in this gripping story that seizes your attention from the very first page."
"If you're a reader who wants to discover an entire family of characters you can fall in love with, this is the series for you." – Authors to Watch
Pierce is a rough man, but happy in his new life as a Special Agent. Tasked with defending the rights of the federal government, Pierce is a cunning gunslinger always ready to tackle the next job. That is, until he finds out that his new job involves Mollie Jamison.

Mollie can be a lot to handle. Headstrong and independent, Mollie has chosen a life of danger and intrigue guaranteed to prove her liquor-loving father wrong. She will make something of herself, and no one, not even arrogant Pierce MacLaren, will stand in her way.

A secret mission brings them together, but will their attraction to each other prove deadly in their hunt for justice? The payoff for success is high, much higher than any assignment either has taken before. But will the damage to their hearts and souls be too much to bear? Can Pierce and Mollie find a way to overcome their misgivings and work together as one?

Second Summer – Book One
MacLarens of Fire Mountain Contemporary Romance Series
"In this passionate Contemporary Romance, author Shirleen Davies introduces her readers to the modern day MacLarens starting with Heath MacLaren, the head of the family."
The Chairman of both the MacLaren Cattle Co. and MacLaren Land Development, Heath MacLaren is a success professionally—his personal life is another matter. *Following a divorce after a long, loveless marriage, Heath spends his time with women who are beautiful and passionate, yet unable to provide what he longs for . . .*

Heath has never experienced love even though he witnesses it every day between his younger brother, Jace, and wife, Caroline. He wants what they have, yet spends his time with women too young to understand what drives him and too focused on themselves to be true companions. *It's been two years since Annie's husband died, leaving her to build a new life. He was her soul mate and confidante.*

She has no desire to find a replacement, yet longs for male friendship.

Annie's closest friend in Fire Mountain, Caroline MacLaren, is determined to see Annie come out of her shell after almost two years of mourning. A chance meeting with Heath turns into an offer to be a part of the MacLaren Foundation Board and an opportunity for a life outside her home sanctuary which has also become her prison. The platonic friendship that builds between Annie and Heath points to a future where each may rely on the other without the bonds a romance would entail.

However, without consciously seeking it, each yearns for more . . .

The MacLaren Development Company is booming with Heath at the helm. His meetings at a partner company with the young, beautiful marketing director, who makes no secret of her desire for him, are a temptation. But is she the type of woman he truly wants?

Annie's acceptance of the deep, yet passionless, friendship with Heath sustains her, lulling her to believe it is all she needs. At least until Heath drops a bombshell, forcing Annie to realize that what she took for friendship is actually a deep, lasting love. One she doesn't want to lose.

Each must decide to settle—or fight for it all.

Hard Landing – Book Two
MacLarens of Fire Mountain Contemporary Romance Series

Trey MacLaren is a confident, poised Navy pilot. He's focused, loyal, ethical, and a natural leader. He is also on his way to what he hopes will be a lasting relationship and marriage with fellow pilot, Jesse Evans.

Jesse has always been driven. Her graduation from the Naval Academy and acceptance into the pilot training program are all she thought she wanted—until she discovered love with Trey MacLaren

Trey and Jesse's lives are filled with fast flying, friends, and the demands of their military careers. Lives each has settled into with a passion. At least until the day Trey receives a letter that could change his and Jesse's lives forever.

It's been over two years since Trey has seen the woman in Pensacola. Her unexpected letter stuns him and pushes Jesse into a tailspin from which she might not pull back.

Each must make a choice. Will the choice Trey makes cause him to lose Jesse forever? Will she follow her heart or her head as she fights for a chance to save the love she's found? Will their independent decisions collide, forcing them to give up on a life together?

One More Day – Book Three
MacLarens of Fire Mountain Contemporary Romance Series

Cameron "Cam" Sinclair is smart, driven, and dedicated, with an easygoing temperament that belies his strong will and the personal ambitions he holds close. Besides his family, his job as head of IT at the MacLaren Cattle Company and his position as a Search and Rescue volunteer are all he needs to make him happy. At least that's what he thinks until he meets, and is instantly drawn to, fellow SAR volunteer, Lainey Devlin.

Lainey is compassionate, independent, and ready to break away from her manipulative and controlling fiancé. Just as her decision is made, she's called into a major search and rescue effort, where once again, her path crosses with the intriguing, and much too handsome, Cam Sinclair. But Lainey's plans are set. An opportunity to buy a flourishing preschool in northern Arizona is her chance to make a fresh start, and nothing, not even her fierce attraction to Cam Sinclair, will impede her plans.

As Lainey begins to settle into her new life, an unexpected danger arises —threats from an unknown assailant—someone who doesn't believe she belongs in Fire Mountain. The more Lainey begins to love her new home, the greater the danger becomes. Can she accept the help and protection Cam offers while ignoring her consuming desire for him?

Even if Lainey accepts her attraction to Cam, will he ever be able to come to terms with his own driving ambition and allow himself to consider a different life than the one he's always pictured? A life with the one woman who offers more than he'd ever hoped to find?

All Your Nights – Book Four
MacLarens of Fire Mountain Contemporary Romance Series
"Romance, adventure, cowboys, suspense— everything you want in a contemporary western romance novel."
Kade Taylor likes living on the edge. As an undercover agent for the DEA and a former Special Ops team member, his current assignment seems tame—keep tabs on a bookish Ph.D. candidate the agency believes is connected to a ruthless drug cartel.

Brooke Sinclair is weeks away from obtaining her goal of a doctoral degree. She spends time finalizing her presentation and relaxing with another student who seems to want nothing more than her friendship. That's fine with Brooke. Her last serious relationship ended in a broken engagement.

Her future is set, safe and peaceful, just as she's always planned—until Agent Taylor informs her she's under suspicion for illegal drug activities.

Kade and his DEA team obtain evidence which exonerates Brooke while placing her in danger from those who sought to use her. As Kade races to take down the drug cartel while protecting Brooke, he must also find common ground with the former suspect—a woman he desires with increasing intensity.

At odds with her better judgment, Brooke finds the more time she spends with Kade, the more she's attracted to the complex, multi-faceted agent. But Kade holds secrets he knows Brooke will never understand or accept.

Can Kade keep Brooke safe while coming to terms with his past, or will he stay silent, ruining any future with the woman his heart can't let go?

Always Love You– Book Five
MacLarens of Fire Mountain Contemporary Romance Series
"Romance, adventure, motorcycles, cowboys, suspense—everything you want in a contemporary western romance novel."
Eric Sinclair loves his bachelor status. His work at MacLaren Enterprises leaves him with plenty of time to ride his horse as well as his Harley...and date beautiful women without a thought to commitment.

Amber Anderson is the new person at MacLaren Enterprises. Her passion for marketing landed her what she believes to be the perfect job—until she steps into her first meeting to find the man she left, but still loves, sitting at the management table—his disdain for her clear.

Eric won't allow the past to taint his professional behavior, nor will he repeat his mistakes with Amber, even though love for her pulses through him as strong as ever.

As they strive to mold a working relationship, unexpected danger confronts those close to them, pitting the MacLarens and Sinclairs against an evil who stalks one member but threatens them all.

Eric can't get the memories of their passionate past out of his mind, while Amber wrestles with feelings she thought long buried. Will they be able to put the past behind them to reclaim the love lost years before?

Hearts Don't Lie– Book Six
MacLarens of Fire Mountain Contemporary Romance Series

Mitch MacLaren has reasons for avoiding relationships, and in his opinion, they're pretty darn good. As the new president of RTC Bucking Bulls, difficult challenges occur daily. He certainly doesn't need another one in the form of a fiery, blue-eyed, redhead.

Dana Ballard's new job forces her to work with the one MacLaren who can't seem to get over himself and lighten up. Their verbal sparring is second nature and entertaining until the night of Mitch's departure when he surprises her with a dare she doesn't refuse.

With his assignment in Fire Mountain over, Mitch is free to return to Montana and run the business his father helped start. The glitch in his enthusiasm has to do with one irreversible mistake—the dare Dana didn't ignore. Now, for reasons that confound him, he just can't let it go.

Working together is a circumstance neither wants, but both must accept. As their attraction grows, so do the accidents and strange illnesses of the animals RTC depends on to stay in business. Mitch's total focus should be on finding the reasons and people behind the incidents. Instead, he finds himself torn between his unwanted desire for Dana and the business which is his life.

In his mind, a simple proposition can solve one problem. Will Dana make the smart move and walk away? Or take the gamble and expose her heart?

No Getting Over You— Book Seven
MacLarens of Fire Mountain Contemporary Romance Series

Cassie MacLaren has come a long way since being dumped by her long-time boyfriend, a man she believed to be her future. Successful in her job at MacLaren Enterprises, dreaming of one day leading one of the divisions, she's moved on to start a new relationship, having little time to dwell on past mistakes.

Matt Garner loves his job as rodeo representative for Double Ace Bucking Stock. Busy days and constant travel leave no time for anything more than the occasional short-term relationship—which is just the way he likes it. He's come to accept the regret of leaving the woman he loved for the pro rodeo circuit.
The future is set for both, until a chance meeting ignites long buried emotions neither is willing to face.

Forced to work together, their attraction grows, even as multiple arson fires threaten Cassie's new home of Cold Creek, Colorado. Although Cassie believes the danger from the fires is remote, she knows the danger Matt poses to her heart is real.

While fighting his renewed feelings for Cassie, Matt focuses on a new and unexpected opportunity offered by MacLaren Enterprises—an opportunity that will put him on a direct collision course with Cassie.

Will pride and self-preservation control their future? Or will one be strong enough to make the first move, risking everything, including their heart?

Redemption's Edge – Book One
Redemption Mountain – Historical Western Romance Series

"A heartwarming, passionate story of loss, forgiveness, and redemption set in the untamed frontier during the tumultuous years following the Civil War. Ms. Davies' engaging and complex characters draw you in from the start, creating an exciting introduction to this new historical western romance series."
"Redemption's Edge is a strong and engaging introduction to her new historical western romance series."
Dax Pelletier is ready for a new life, far away from the one he left behind in Savannah following the South's devastating defeat in the Civil War. The ex-Confederate general wants nothing more to do with commanding men and confronting the tough truths of leadership.

Rachel Davenport possesses skills unlike those of her Boston socialite peers—skills honed as a nurse in field hospitals during the Civil War. Eschewing her northeastern suitors and changed by the carnage she's seen, Rachel decides to accept her uncle's invitation to assist him at his clinic in the dangerous and wild frontier of Montana.

Now a Texas Ranger, a promise to a friend takes Dax and his brother, Luke, to the untamed territory of Montana. He'll fulfill his oath and return to Austin, at least that's what he believes.

The small town of Splendor is what Rachel needs after life in a large city. In a few short months, she's grown to love the people as well as the majestic beauty of the untamed frontier. She's settled into a life unlike any she has ever thought possible.

Thinking his battle days are over, he now faces dangers of a different kind—one by those from his past who seek vengeance, and another from Rachel, the woman who's captured his heart.

Wildfire Creek – Book Two
Redemption Mountain – Historical Western Romance Series

"A passionate story of rebuilding lives, working to find a place in the wild frontier, and building new lives in the years following the American Civil War. A rugged, heartwarming story of choices and love in the continuing saga of Redemption Mountain."

Luke Pelletier is settling into his new life as a rancher and occasional Pinkerton Agent, leaving his past as an ex-Confederate major and Texas Ranger far behind. He wants nothing more than to work the ranch, charm the ladies, and live a life of carefree bachelorhood.

Ginny Sorensen has accepted her responsibility as the sole provider for herself and her younger sister. The desire to continue their journey to Oregon is crushed when the need for food and shelter keeps them in the growing frontier town of Splendor, Montana, forcing Ginny to accept work as a server in the local saloon.

Luke has never met a woman as lovely and unspoiled as Ginny. He longs to know her, yet fears his wild ways and unsettled nature aren't what she deserves. She's a girl you marry, but that is nowhere in Luke's plans.

Complicating their tenuous friendship, a twist in circumstances forces Ginny closer to the man she most wants to avoid—the man who can destroy her dreams, and who's captured her heart.

Believing his bachelor status firm, Luke moves from danger to adventure, never dreaming each step he takes brings him closer to his true destiny and a life much different from what he imagines.

Sunrise Ridge – Book Three
Redemption Mountain – Historical Western Romance Series

"The author has a talent for bringing the historical west to life, realistically and vividly, and doesn't shy away from some of the harder aspects of frontier life, even though it's fiction. Recommended to readers who like sweeping western historical romances that are grounded with memorable, likeable characters and a strong sense of place."

Noah Brandt is a successful blacksmith and businessman in Splendor, Montana, with few ties to his past as an ex-Union Army major and sharpshooter. Quiet and hardworking, his biggest challenge is controlling his strong desire for a woman he believes is beyond his reach.

Abigail Tolbert is tired of being under her father's thumb while at the same time, being pushed away by the one man she desires. Determined to build a new life outside the control of her wealthy father, she finds work and sets out to shape a life on her own terms.

Noah has made too many mistakes with Abby to have any hope of getting her back. Even with the changes in her life, including the distance she's built with her father, he can't keep himself from believing he'll never be good enough to claim her.

Unexpected dangers, including a twist of fate for Abby, change both their lives, making the tentative steps they've taken to build a relationship a distant hope. As Noah battles his past as well as the threats to Abby, she fights for a future with the only man she will ever love.

Dixie Moon – Book Four
Redemption Mountain – Historical Western Romance Series

Gabe Evans is a man of his word with strong convictions and steadfast loyalty. As the sheriff of Splendor, Montana, the ex-Union Colonel and oldest of four boys from an affluent family, Gabe understands the meaning of responsibility. The last thing he wants is another commitment—especially of the female variety.

Until he meets Lena Campanel…

Lena's past is one she intends to keep buried. Overcoming a childhood of setbacks and obstacles, she and her friend, Nick, have succeeded in creating a life of financial success and devout loyalty to one another.

When an unexpected death leaves Gabe the sole heir of a considerable estate, partnering with Nick and Lena is a lucrative decision...forcing Gabe and Lena to work together. As their desire grows, Lena refuses to let down her guard, vowing to keep her past hidden—even from a perfect man like Gabe.

But secrets never stay buried...

When revealed, Gabe realizes Lena's secrets are deeper than he ever imagined. For a man of his character, deception and lies of omission aren't negotiable. Will he be able to forgive the deceit? Or is the damage too great to ever repair?

Survivor Pass – Book Five
Redemption Mountain – Historical Western Romance Series

He thought he'd found a quiet life...

Cash Coulter settled into a life far removed from his days of fighting for the South and crossing the country as a bounty hunter. Now a deputy sheriff, Cash wants nothing more than to buy some land, raise cattle, and build a simple life in the frontier town of Splendor, Montana. But his whole world shifts when his gaze lands on the most captivating woman he's ever seen. And the feeling appears to be mutual.

But nothing is as it seems...

Alison McGrath moved from her home in Kentucky to the rugged mountains of Montana for one reason—to find the man responsible for murdering her brother. Despite using a false identity to avoid any tie to her brother's name, the citizens of Splendor have no intention of sharing their knowledge about the bank robbery which killed her only sibling. Alison knows her circle of lies can't end well, and her growing for Cash threatens to weaken the revenge which drives her.

And the troubles are mounting...

There is danger surrounding them both—men who seek vengeance as a way to silence the past...by any means necessary.

Reclaiming Love – Book One, A Novella
Peregrine Bay – Contemporary Romance Series
Adam Monroe has seen his share of setbacks. Now he's back in Peregrine Bay, looking for a new life and second chance. Julia Kerrigan's life rebounded after the sudden betrayal of the one man she ever loved. As president of a success real estate company, she's built a new life and future, pushing the painful past behind her.
Adam's reason for accepting the job as the town's new Police Chief can be explained in one word—Julia. He wants her back and will do whatever is necessary to achieve his goal, even knowing his biggest hurdle is the woman he still loves. As they begin to reconnect, a terrible scandal breaks loose with Julia and Adam at the center.
Will the threat to their lives and reputations destroy their fledgling romance? Can Adam identify and eliminate the danger to Julia before he's had a chance to reclaim her love?

Our Kind of Love – Book Two
Peregrine Bay – Contemporary Romance Series
Selena Kerrigan is content with a life filled with work and family, never feeling the need to take a chance on a relationship—until she steps into a social world inhabited by a man with dark hair and penetrating blue eyes. Eyes that are fixed on her.

Lincoln Caldwell is a man satisfied with his life. Transitioning from an enviable career as a Navy SEAL to becoming a successful entrepreneur, his days focus on growing his security firm, spending his nights with whomever he chooses. Committing to one woman isn't on the horizon—until a captivating woman with caramel eyes sends his personal life into a tailspin.

Believing her identity remains a secret, Selena returns to work, ready to forget about running away from the bed she never should have gone near. She's prepared to put the colossal error, as well as the man she'll never see again, behind her.

Too bad the object of her lapse in judgment doesn't feel the same.

Linc is good at tracking his targets, and Selena is now at the top of his list. It's amazing how a pair of sandals and only a first name can say so much.

As he pursues the woman he can't rid from his mind, a series of cyber-attacks hit his business, threatening its hard-won success. Worse, and unbeknownst to most, Linc harbors a secret—one with the potential to alter his life, along with those he's close to, in ways he could never imagine.
Our Kind of Love, Book Two in the Peregrine Bay Contemporary Romance series, is a full-length novel with an HEA and no cliffhanger.

Colin's Quest – Book One
MacLarens of Boundary Mountain – Historical Western Romance Series
For An Undying Love...
When Colin MacLaren headed west on a wagon train, he hoped to find adventure and perhaps a little danger in untamed California. He never expected to meet the girl he would love forever. He also never expected her to be the

daughter of his family's age-old enemy, but Sarah was a MacGregor and the anger he anticipated soon became a reality. Her father would not be swayed, vehemently refusing to allow marriage to a MacLaren.

Time Has No Effect…
Forced apart for five years, Sarah never forgot Colin—nor did she give up on his promise to come for her. Carrying the brooch he gave her as proof of their secret betrothal, she scans the trail from California, waiting for Colin to claim her. Unfortunately, her father has other plans.

And Enemies Hold No Power.
Nothing can stop Colin from locating Sarah. Not outlaws, runaways, or miles of difficult trails. However, reuniting is only the beginning. Together they must find the courage to fight the men who would keep them apart—and conquer the challenge of uniting two independent hearts.

Find all of my books at:
http://www.shirleendavies.com/books.html

www.ingramcontent.com/pod-product-compliance
Lightning Source LLC
Chambersburg PA
CBHW060800210726
48292CB00013B/944